George Silverman's Explanation

followed by

Hunted Down

and

Holiday Romance

Charles Dickens

ALMA CLASSICS

ALMA CLASSICS LTD
London House
243-253 Lower Mortlake Road
Richmond
Surrey TW9 2LL
United Kingdom
www.almaclassics.com

George Silverman's Explanation first published in 1868
Hunted Down first published in 1859
Holiday Romance first published in 1868
This collection first published by Alma Books Ltd in 2015

Cover design © Marina Rodrigues

Extra Material © Alma Classics Ltd

Printed and bound by CPI Group (UK) Ltd, Croydon, CR0 4YY

ISBN: 978-1-84749-402-3

Contents

Charles Dickens (1812–70)

John Dickens,
Charles's father

Elizabeth Dickens,
Charles's mother

Catherine Dickens,
Charles's wife

Ellen Ternan

1 Mile End Terrace, Portsmouth, Dickens's birthplace (above left),
48 Doughty Street, London, Dickens's home 1837–39 (above right)
and Tavistock House, London, Dickens's residence 1851–60 (below)

Gad's Hill Place, Kent, where Dickens lived from 1857 to 1870 (above) and the author in his study at Gad's Hill Place (below)

George Silverman's
Explanation

George Silverman's
Explanation

First Chapter

I T HAPPENED in this wise—
But, sitting with my pen in my hand looking at those words again, without descrying any hint in them of the words that should follow, it comes into my mind that they have an abrupt appearance. They may serve, however, if I let them remain, to suggest how very difficult I find it to begin to explain my explanation. An uncouth phrase: and yet I do not see my way to a better.

Second Chapter

I T HAPPENED in *this* wise—
But, looking at those words, and comparing them with my former opening, I find they are the selfsame words repeated. This is the more surprising to me, because I employ them in quite a new connection. For indeed I declare that my intention was to discard the commencement I first had in my thoughts, and to give the preference to another of an entirely different nature, dating my explanation from an anterior period of my life. I will make a third trial, without erasing this second failure, protesting that it is not my design to conceal any of my infirmities, whether they be of head or heart.

Third Chapter

NOT AS YET DIRECTLY aiming at how it came to pass, I will come upon it by degrees. The natural manner, after all, for God knows that is how it came upon me.

My parents were in a miserable condition of life, and my infant home was a cellar in Preston. I recollect the sound of father's Lancashire clogs on the street pavement above as being different in my young hearing from the sound of all other clogs; and I recollect, that, when mother came down the cellar steps, I used tremblingly to speculate on her feet having a good or an ill-tempered look – on her knees – on her waist – until finally her face came into view, and settled the question. From this it will be seen that I was timid, and that the cellar steps were steep, and that the doorway was very low.

Mother had the gripe and clutch of poverty upon her face, upon her figure, and not least of all upon her voice. Her sharp and high-pitched words were squeezed out of her, as by the compression of bony fingers on a leathern bag; and she had a way of rolling her eyes about and about the cellar, as she scolded, that was gaunt and hungry. Father, with his shoulders rounded, would sit quiet on a three-legged stool, looking at the empty grate, until she would pluck the stool from under him, and bid him go bring some money home. Then he would dismally ascend the steps; and I, holding my ragged shirt and trousers together with a hand (my only braces), would feint and dodge from Mother's pursuing grasp at my hair.

A worldly little devil was mother's usual name for me. Whether I cried for that I was in the dark, or for that it was cold, or for that I was hungry, or whether I squeezed myself into a warm corner when there was a fire, or ate voraciously when there was food, she would still say, "O you worldly little devil!" And the sting of it was that I quite well knew myself to be a worldly little devil. Worldly as to wanting to be housed and warmed, worldly as to wanting to be fed, worldly as to the greed with which I inwardly compared how much I got of those good things with how much Father and Mother got when, rarely, those good things were going.

Sometimes they both went away seeking work; and then I would be locked up in the cellar for a day or two at a time. I was at my worldliest then. Left alone, I yielded myself up to a worldly yearning for enough of anything (except misery), and for the death of Mother's father, who was a machine-maker at Birmingham, and on whose decease, I had heard Mother say, she would come into a whole courtful of houses "if she had her rights". Worldly little devil, I would stand about, musingly fitting my cold bare feet into cracked bricks and crevices of the damp cellar floor – walking over my grandfather's body, so to speak, into the courtful of houses, and selling them for meat and drink, and clothes to wear.

At last a change came down into our cellar. The universal change came down even as low as that – so will it mount to any height on which a human creature can perch – and brought other changes with it.

We had a heap of I don't know what foul litter in the darkest corner, which we called "the bed". For three days Mother lay upon it without getting up, and then began at times to laugh. If I had ever heard her laugh before, it had been so seldom that the strange sound frightened me. It frightened Father too; and we took it by turns to give her water. Then she began to move her head from side to side and sing. After that, she getting no better, Father fell a-laughing and a-singing; and then there was only I to give them both water, and they both died.

Fourth Chapter

WHEN I WAS LIFTED OUT of the cellar by two men, of whom one came peeping down alone first, and ran away and brought the other, I could hardly bear the light of the street. I was sitting in the roadway, blinking at it, and at a ring of people collected around me, but not close to me, when, true to my character of worldly little devil, I broke silence by saying, "I am hungry and thirsty!"

"Does he know they are dead?" asked one of another.

"Do you know your father and mother are both dead of fever?" asked a third of me severely.

"I don't know what it is to be dead. I supposed it meant that when the cup rattled against their teeth and the water spilt over them. I am hungry and thirsty." That was all I had to say about it.

The ring of people widened outward from the inner side as I looked around me; and I smelt vinegar, and what I know to be camphor, thrown in towards where I sat. Presently someone put a great vessel of smoking vinegar on the ground near me; and then they all looked at me in silent horror as I ate and drank of what was brought for me. I knew at the time they had a horror of me, but I couldn't help it.

I was still eating and drinking, and a murmur of discussion had begun to arise respecting what was to be done with me next, when I heard a cracked voice somewhere in the ring say, "My name is Hawkyard, Mr Verity Hawkyard, of West Bromwich." Then the ring split in one place, and a yellow-faced, peak-nosed gentleman, clad all in iron-grey to his gaiters, pressed forward with a police-man and another official of some sort. He came forward close to the vessel of smoking vinegar; from which he sprinkled himself carefully, and me copiously.

"He had a grandfather at Birmingham, this young boy, who is just dead too," said Mr Hawkyard.

I turned my eyes upon the speaker, and said in a ravening manner, "Where's his houses?"

"Hah! Horrible worldliness on the edge of the grave," said Mr Hawkyard, casting more of the vinegar over me, as if to get my devil out of me. "I have undertaken a slight – a ve-ry slight – trust in behalf of this boy; quite a voluntary trust: a matter of mere honour, if not of mere sentiment: still I have taken it upon myself, and it shall be (Oh, yes, it shall be!) discharged."

The bystanders seemed to form an opinion of this gentleman much more favourable than their opinion of me.

"He shall be taught," said Mr Hawkyard, "(Oh, yes, he shall be taught!) – but what is to be done with him for the present? He may be infected. He may disseminate infection." The ring widened considerably. "What is to be done with him?"

He held some talk with the two officials, I could distinguish no word save "Farmhouse". There was another sound several times repeated, which was wholly meaningless in my ears then, but which I knew afterwards to be "Hoghton Towers".

"Yes," said Mr Hawkyard. "I think that sounds promising; I think that sounds hopeful. And he can be put by himself in a ward, for a night or two, you say?"

It seemed to be the police officer who had said so; for it was he who replied, "Yes!" It was he, too, who finally took me by the arm, and walked me before him through the streets, into a whitewashed room in a bare building, where I had a chair to sit in, a table to sit at, an iron bedstead and good mattress to lie upon, and a rug and blanket to cover me. Where I had enough to eat too, and was shown how to clean the tin porringer in which it was conveyed to me, until it was as good as a looking glass. Here, likewise, I was put in a bath, and had new clothes brought to me; and my old rags were burnt, and I was camphored and vinegared and disinfected in a variety of ways.

When all this was done – I don't know in how many days or how few, but it matters not – Mr Hawkyard stepped in at the door, remaining close to it, and said, "Go and stand against the opposite wall, George Silverman. As far off as you can. That'll do. How do you feel?"

I told him that I didn't feel cold, and didn't feel hungry, and didn't feel thirsty. That was the whole round of human feelings, as far as I knew, except the pain of being beaten.

"Well," said he, "you are going, George, to a healthy farmhouse to be purified. Keep in the air there as much as you can. Live an out-of-door life there, until you are fetched away. You had better not say much – in fact, you had better be very careful not to say anything – about what your parents died of, or they might not like to take you in. Behave well, and I'll put you to school – oh, yes! – I'll put you to school, though I'm not obligated to do it. I am a servant of the Lord, George; and I have been a good servant to Him, I have, these five-and-thirty years. The Lord has had a good servant in me, and He knows it."

What I then supposed him to mean by this I cannot imagine. As little do I know when I began to comprehend that he was a prominent member of some obscure denomination or congregation, every member of which held forth to the rest when so inclined, and among whom he was called Brother Hawkyard. It was enough for me to know, on that day in the ward, that the farmer's cart was waiting for me at the street corner. I was not slow to get into it; for it was the first ride I ever had in my life.

It made me sleepy, and I slept. First I stared at Preston streets as long as they lasted; and, meanwhile, I may have had some small dumb wondering within me whereabouts our cellar was; but I doubt it. Such a worldly little devil was I that I took no thought who would bury Father and Mother, or where they would be buried, or when. The question whether the eating and drinking by day, and the covering by night, would be as good at the farmhouse as at the ward superseded those questions.

The jolting of the cart on a loose stony road awoke me; and I found that we were mounting a steep hill, where the road was a rutty byroad through a field. And so, by fragments of an ancient terrace, and by some rugged outbuildings that had once been fortified and passing under a ruined gateway, we came to the old farmhouse in the thick stone wall outside the old quadrangle of Hoghton Towers: which I looked at like a stupid savage, seeing no specialty in, seeing no antiquity in; assuming all farmhouses to resemble it; assigning the decay I noticed to the one potent cause of all ruin that I knew – poverty; eyeing the pigeons in their flights, the cattle in their stalls, the ducks in the pond and the fowls pecking about the yard, with a hungry hope that plenty of them might be killed for dinner while I stayed there; wondering whether the scrubbed dairy vessels, drying in the sunlight, could be goodly porringers out of which the master ate his belly-filling food, and which he polished when he had done, according to my ward experience; shrinkingly doubtful whether the shadows, passing over that airy height on the bright spring day, were not something in the nature of frowns – sordid, afraid, unadmiring – a small brute to shudder at.

To that time I had never had the faintest impression of duty. I had had no knowledge whatever that there was anything lovely in this life. When I had occasionally slunk up the cellar steps into the street and glared in at shop windows, I had done so with no higher feelings than we may suppose to animate a mangy young dog or wolf cub. It is equally the fact that I had never been alone, in the sense of holding unselfish converse with myself. I had been solitary often enough, but nothing better.

Such was my condition when I sat down to my dinner that day, in the kitchen of the old farmhouse. Such was my condition when I lay on my bed in the old farmhouse that night, stretched out opposite the narrow mullioned window, in the cold light of the moon, like a young vampire.

Fifth Chapter

WHAT DO I KNOW NOW of Hoghton Towers? Very little; for I have been gratefully unwilling to disturb my first impressions. A house, centuries old, on high ground a mile or so removed from the road between Preston and Blackburn, where the first James of England, in his hurry to make money by making baronets, perhaps made some of those remunerative dignitaries. A house, centuries old, deserted and falling to pieces, its woods and gardens long since grassland or ploughed up, the Rivers Ribble and Darwen glancing below it and a vague haze of smoke, against which not even the supernatural prescience of the first Stuart could foresee a counterblast, hinting at steam power, powerful in two distances.

What did I know then of Hoghton Towers? When I first peeped in at the gate of the lifeless quadrangle, and started from the mouldering statue becoming visible to me like its guardian ghost; when I stole round by the back of the farmhouse, and got in among the ancient rooms, many of them with their floors and ceilings falling, the beams and rafters hanging dangerously down, the plaster dropping as I trod, the oaken panels stripped away, the windows half walled up, half broken; when I discovered a gallery commanding the old kitchen and looked down between balustrades upon a massive old table and benches, fearing to see I know not what dead-alive creatures come in and seat themselves, and look up with I know not what dreadful eyes, or lack of eyes, at me; when all over the house I was awed by gaps and chinks where the sky stared sorrowfully at me, where the birds passed and the ivy rustled, and the stains of winter weather blotched the rotten floors; when down at the bottom of dark pits of staircase, into which the stairs had sunk, green leaves trembled, butterflies fluttered and bees hummed in and out through the broken doorways; when encircling the whole ruin were sweet scents and sights of fresh green growth, and ever-renewing life, that I had never dreamt of − I say, when I passed into such clouded perception of these things as my dark soul could compass, what did I know then of Hoghton Towers?

I have written that the sky stared sorrowfully at me. Therein have I anticipated the answer. I knew that all these things looked sorrowfully at me; that they seemed to sigh or whisper, not without pity for me, "Alas! Poor worldly little devil!"

There were two or three rats at the bottom of one of the smaller pits of broken staircase when I craned over and looked in. They were scuffling for some prey that was there; and, when they started and hid themselves close together in the dark, I thought of the old life (it had grown old already) in the cellar.

How not to be this worldly little devil? How not to have a repugnance towards myself as I had towards the rats? I hid in a corner of one of the smaller chambers, frightened at myself, and crying (it was the first time I had ever cried for any cause not purely physical), and I tried to think about it. One of the farm ploughs came into my range of view just then; and it seemed to help me as it went on with its two horses up and down the field so peacefully and quietly.

There was a girl of about my own age in the farmhouse family, and she sat opposite to me at the narrow table at mealtimes. It had come into my mind, at our first dinner, that she might take the fever from me. The thought had not disquieted me then. I had only speculated how she would look under the altered circumstances, and whether she would die. But it came into my mind now that I might try to prevent her taking the fever by keeping away from her. I knew I should have but scrambling board* if I did; so much the less worldly and less devilish the deed would be, I thought.

From that hour, I withdrew myself at early morning into secret corners of the ruined house, and remained hidden there until she went to bed. At first, when meals were ready, I used to hear them calling me – and then my resolution weakened. But I strengthened it again by going farther off into the ruin, and getting out of hearing. I often watched for her at the dim windows and, when I saw that she was fresh and rosy, felt much happier.

Out of this holding her in my thoughts, to the humanizing of myself, I suppose some childish love arose within me. I felt, in some sort, dignified by the pride of protecting her – by the pride of making the sacrifice for her. As my heart swelled with that new feeling, it insensibly softened about Mother and Father. It seemed to have been frozen before, and now to be thawed. The old ruin and all the lovely things that haunted it were not sorrowful for me only, but sorrowful for Mother and Father as well. Therefore did I cry again, and often too.

The farmhouse family conceived me to be of a morose temper, and were very short with me; though they never stinted me in such broken fare as was to be got out of regular hours. One night when I lifted the kitchen latch at my usual time, Sylvia (that was her pretty name) had but just gone out of the room. Seeing her ascending the opposite stairs, I stood still at the door. She had heard the clink of the latch, and looked round.

"George," she called to me in a pleased voice, "tomorrow is my birthday; and we are to have a fiddler, and there's a party of

boys and girls coming in a cart, and we shall dance. I invite you.
Be sociable for once, George."

"I am very sorry, miss," I answered, "but I... but, no; I can't
come."

"You are a disagreeable, ill-humoured lad," she returned dis-
dainfully, "and I ought not to have asked you. I shall never speak
to you again."

As I stood with my eyes fixed on the fire, after she was gone, I
felt that the farmer bent his brows upon me.

"Eh, lad!" said he. "Sylvy's right. You're as moody and broody
a lad as never I set eyes on yet."

I tried to assure him that I meant no harm; but he only said
coldly, "Maybe not, maybe not! There, get thy supper, get thy
supper – and then thou canst sulk to thy heart's content again."

Ah! If they could have seen me next day, in the ruin, watching
for the arrival of the cart full of merry young guests; if they could
have seen me at night, gliding out from behind the ghostly statue,
listening to the music and the fall of dancing feet and watching
the lighted farmhouse windows from the quadrangle when all the
ruin was dark; if they could have read my heart, as I crept up to
bed by the back way, comforting myself with the reflection, "They
will take no hurt from me" – they would not have thought mine
a morose or an unsocial nature.

It was in these ways that I began to form a shy disposition; to
be of a timidly silent character under misconstruction; to have
an inexpressible, perhaps a morbid dread of ever being sordid or

worldly. It was in these ways that my nature came to shape itself to such a mould, even before it was affected by the influences of the studious and retired life of a poor scholar.

Sixth Chapter

B ROTHER HAWKYARD (as he insisted on my calling him) put me to school, and told me to work my way. "You are all right, George," he said. "I have been the best servant the Lord has had in His service for this five-and-thirty year (oh, I have!); and He knows the value of such a servant as I have been to Him (oh, yes, He does!); and He'll prosper your schooling as a part of my reward. That's what *He*'ll do, George. He'll do it for me."

From the first I could not like this familiar knowledge of the ways of the sublime, inscrutable Almighty, on Brother Hawkyard's part. As I grew a little wiser, and still a little wiser, I liked it less and less. His manner, too, of confirming himself in a parenthesis – as if, knowing himself, he doubted his own word – I found distasteful. I cannot tell how much these dislikes cost me; for I had a dread that they were worldly.

As time went on, I became a foundation boy on a good foundation, and I cost Brother Hawkyard nothing. When I had worked my way so far, I worked yet harder, in the hope of ultimately getting a presentation to college and a fellowship. My health has never been strong (some vapour from the Preston cellar cleaves to me,

I think); and what with much work and some weakness, I came again to be regarded – that is, by my fellow students – as unsocial.

All through my time as a foundation boy, I was within a few miles of Brother Hawkyard's congregation; and whenever I was what we called a leave boy on a Sunday, I went over there at his desire. Before the knowledge became forced upon me that outside their place of meeting these brothers and sisters were no better than the rest of the human family, but on the whole were, to put the case mildly, as bad as most, in respect of giving short weight in their shops, and not speaking the truth – I say, before this knowledge became forced upon me, their prolix addresses, their inordinate conceit, their daring ignorance, their investment of the Supreme Ruler of heaven and earth with their own miserable meannesses and littlenesses, greatly shocked me. Still, as their term for the frame of mind that could not perceive them to be in an exalted state of grace was the "worldly" state, I did for a time suffer tortures under my enquiries of myself whether that young worldly devilish spirit of mine could secretly be lingering at the bottom of my non-appreciation.

Brother Hawkyard was the popular expounder in this assembly, and generally occupied the platform (there was a little platform with a table on it, in lieu of a pulpit) first, on a Sunday afternoon. He was by trade a dry-salter. Brother Gimblet, an elderly man with a crabbed face, a large dog's-eared shirt collar and a spotted blue neckerchief reaching up behind to the crown of his head, was also a dry-salter and an expounder. Brother Gimblet professed

CHARLES DICKENS

the greatest admiration for Brother Hawkyard, but (I had thought more than once) bore him a jealous grudge.

Let whosoever may peruse these lines kindly take the pains here to read twice my solemn pledge that what I write of the language and customs of the congregation in question I write scrupulously, literally, exactly, from the life and the truth.

On the first Sunday after I had won what I had so long tried for, and when it was certain that I was going up to college, Brother Hawkyard concluded a long exhortation thus:

"Well, my friends and fellow sinners, now I told you when I began that I didn't know a word of what I was going to say to you (and no, I did not!), but that it was all one to me, because I knew the Lord would put into my mouth the words I wanted."

("That's it!" from Brother Gimblet.)

"And He did put into my mouth the words I wanted."

("So He did!" from Brother Gimblet.)

"And why?"

("Ah, let's have that!" from Brother Gimblet.)

"Because I have been His faithful servant for five-and-thirty years, and because He knows it. For five-and-thirty years! And He knows it, mind you! I got those words that I wanted on account of my wages. I got 'em from the Lord, my fellow sinners. Down! I said, 'Here's a heap of wages due; let us have something down, on account.' And I got it down, and I paid it over to you; and you won't wrap it up in a napkin, nor yet in a towel, nor yet pocket-ankercher, but you'll put it out at good interest. Very well. Now, my brothers and sisters and fellow sinners, I am going to conclude with a question, and I'll make it so plain (with the help of the Lord, after five-and-thirty years, I should rather hope!) as that the Devil shall not be able to confuse it in your heads – which he would be overjoyed to do." ("Just his way. Crafty old blackguard!" from Brother Gimblet.)

"And the question is this: are the angels learned?"

("Not they. Not a bit on it!" from Brother Gimblet, with the greatest confidence.)

"Not they. And where's the proof? Sent ready-made by the hand of the Lord. Why, there's one among us here now that has got all the learning that can be crammed into him. *I* got him all the learning that could be crammed into him. His grandfather" (this I had never heard before) "was a brother of ours. He was Brother Parksop. That's what he was. Parksop, Brother Parksop. His worldly name was Parksop, and he was a brother of this brotherhood. Then wasn't he Brother Parksop?"

("Must be. Couldn't help hisself!" from Brother Gimblet.)

"Well, he left that one now here present among us to the care of a brother sinner of his (and that brother sinner, mind you, was a sinner of a bigger size in his time than any of you; praise the Lord!), Brother Hawkyard. Me. *I* got him without fee or reward – without a morsel of myrrh, or frankincense, nor yet amber, letting alone the honeycomb – all the learning that could be crammed into him. Has it brought him into our temple, in the spirit? No. Have we had any ignorant brothers and sisters that didn't know round O from crooked S come in among us meanwhile? Many. Then the angels are *not* learned; then they don't so much as know their alphabet. And now, my friends and fellow sinners, having brought it to that, perhaps some brother present – perhaps you, Brother Gimblet – will pray a bit for us?"

Brother Gimblet undertook the sacred function, after having drawn his sleeve across his mouth and muttered, "Well! I don't know as I see my way to hitting any of you quite in the right place neither." He said this with a dark smile, and then began to bellow. What we were specially to be preserved from, according to his solicitations, was despoilment of the orphan, suppression of testamentary intentions on the part of a father or (say) grandfather, appropriation of the orphan's house property, feigning to give in charity to the wronged one from whom we withheld his due; and that class of sins. He ended with the petition "Give us peace!" which, speaking for myself, was very much needed after twenty minutes of his bellowing.

Even though I had not seen him when he rose from his knees, steaming with perspiration, glance at Brother Hawkyard, and even though I had not heard Brother Hawkyard's tone of congratulating him on the vigour with which he had roared, I should have detected a malicious application in this prayer. Unformed suspicions to a similar effect had sometimes passed through my mind in my earlier schooldays, and had always caused me great distress; for they were worldly in their nature, and wide, very wide, of the spirit that had drawn me from Sylvia. They were sordid suspicions, without a shadow of proof. They were worthy to have originated in the unwholesome cellar. They were not only without proof, but against proof; for was I not myself a living proof of what Brother Hawkyard had done? And without him, how should I ever have seen the sky look sorrowfully down upon that wretched boy at Hoghton Towers?

Although the dread of a relapse into a stage of savage selfishness was less strong upon me as I approached manhood, and could act in an increased degree for myself, yet I was always on my guard against any tendency to such relapse. After getting these suspicions under my feet, I had been troubled by not being able to like Brother Hawkyard's manner, or his professed religion. So it came about that, as I walked back that Sunday evening, I thought it would be an act of reparation for any such injury my struggling thoughts had unwillingly done him, if I wrote, and placed in his hands, before going to college, a full acknowledgment of his goodness to me, and an ample tribute of thanks. It might serve as an implied vindication of him against any dark scandal from a rival brother and expounder, or from any other quarter.

Accordingly, I wrote the document with much care. I may add with much feeling too; for it affected me as I went on. Having no set studies to pursue, in the brief interval between leaving the Foundation and going to Cambridge, I determined to walk out to his place of business and give it into his own hands.

It was a winter afternoon, when I tapped at the door of his little counting house, which was at the farther end of his long, low shop. As I did so (having entered by the backyard, where casks and boxes were taken in, and where there was the inscription, "Private way to the counting house"), a shopman called to me from the counter that he was engaged.

"Brother Gimblet" (said the shopman, who was one of the brotherhood) "is with him."

I thought this all the better for my purpose, and made bold to tap again. They were talking in a low tone, and money was passing, for I heard it being counted out.

"Who is it?" asked Brother Hawkyard sharply.

"George Silverman," I answered, holding the door open. "May I come in?"

Both brothers seemed so astounded to see me that I felt shyer than usual. But they looked quite cadaverous in the early gaslight, and perhaps that accidental circumstance exaggerated the expression of their faces.

"What is the matter?" asked Brother Hawkyard.

"Ay! What is the matter?" asked Brother Gimblet.

"Nothing at all," I said, diffidently producing my document: "I am only the bearer of a letter from myself."

"From yourself, George?" cried Brother Hawkyard.

"And to you," said I.

"And to me, George?"

He turned paler, and opened it hurriedly, but looking over it, and seeing generally what it was, became less hurried, recovered his colour, and said, "Praise the Lord!"

"That's it!" cried Brother Gimblet. "Well put! Amen."

Brother Hawkyard then said, in a livelier strain, "You must know, George, that Brother Gimblet and I are going to make our two businesses one. We are going into partnership. We are settling it now. Brother Gimblet is to take one clear half of the profits (oh, yes! He shall have it; he shall have it to the last farthing)."

"DV!"* said Brother Gimblet, with his right fist firmly clinched on his right leg.

"There is no objection," pursued Brother Hawkyard, "to my reading this aloud, George?"

As it was what I expressly desired should be done, after yesterday's prayer, I more than readily begged him to read it aloud. He did so, and Brother Gimblet listened with a crabbed smile.

"It was in a good hour that I came here," he said, wrinkling up his eyes. "It was in a good hour, likewise, that I was moved yesterday to depict for the terror of evildoers a character the direct opposite of Brother Hawkyard's. But it was the Lord that done it: I felt him at it while I was perspiring."

After that it was proposed by both of them that I should attend the congregation once more before my final departure. What my shy reserve would undergo, from being expressly preached at and prayed at, I knew beforehand. But I reflected that it would be for the last time, and that it might add to the weight of my letter. It was well known to the brothers and sisters that there was no place taken for me in *their* paradise; and if I showed this last token of deference to Brother Hawkyard, notoriously in despite of my own

sinful inclinations, it might go some little way in aid of my statement that he had been good to me, and that I was grateful to him.
Merely stipulating, therefore, that no express endeavour should
be made for my conversion – which would involve the rolling of
several brothers and sisters on the floor, declaring that they felt all
their sins in a heap on their left side, weighing so many pounds
avoirdupois, as I knew from what I had seen of those repulsive
mysteries – I promised.

Since the reading of my letter, Brother Gimblet had been at intervals wiping one eye with an end of his spotted-blue neckerchief,
and grinning to himself. It was, however, a habit that brother had
to grin in an ugly manner even when expounding. I call to mind
a delighted snarl with which he used to detail from the platform
the torments reserved for the wicked (meaning all human creation
except the brotherhood), as being remarkably hideous.

I left the two to settle their articles of partnership and count
money, and I never saw them again but on the following Sunday.
Brother Hawkyard died within two or three years, leaving all he
possessed to Brother Gimblet, in virtue of a will dated (as I have
been told) that very day.

Now I was so far at rest with myself, when Sunday came, knowing that I had conquered my own mistrust and righted Brother
Hawkyard in the jaundiced vision of a rival, that I went, even to
that coarse chapel, in a less sensitive state than usual. How could
I foresee that the delicate, perhaps the diseased, corner of my
mind, where I winced and shrunk when it was touched, or was

even approached, would be handled as the theme of the whole proceedings?

On this occasion it was assigned to Brother Hawkyard to pray, and to Brother Gimblet to preach. The prayer was to open the ceremonies; the discourse was to come next. Brothers Hawkyard and Gimblet were both on the platform; Brother Hawkyard on his knees at the table, unmusically ready to pray; Brother Gimblet sitting against the wall, grinningly ready to preach.

"Let us offer up the sacrifice of prayer, my brothers and sisters and fellow sinners." Yes; but it was I who was the sacrifice. It was our poor, sinful, worldly-minded brother here present who was wrestled for. The now opening career of this our unawakened brother might lead to his becoming a minister of what was called "the church". That was what *he* looked to. The church. Not the chapel, Lord. The church. No rectors, no vicars, no archdeacons, no bishops, no archbishops in the chapel, but – O Lord! – many such in the church. Protect our sinful brother from his love of lucre. Cleanse from our unawakened brother's breast his sin of worldly-mindedness. The prayer said infinitely more in words, but nothing more to any intelligible effect.

Then Brother Gimblet came forward, and took (as I knew he would) the text "My kingdom is not of this world". Ah! But whose was, my fellow sinners? Whose? Why, our brother's here present was. The only kingdom he had an idea of was of this world. ("That's it!" from several of the congregation.) What did the woman do when she lost the piece of money? Went and looked for it. What should our brother do when he lost his way? ("Go and look for it," from a sister.) Go and look for it, true. But must he look for it in the right direction, or in the wrong? ("In the right," from a brother.) There spake the prophets! He must look for it in the right direction, or he couldn't find it. But he had turned his back upon the right direction, and he wouldn't find it. Now, my fellow sinners, to show you the difference betwixt worldly-mindedness and unworldly-mindedness, betwixt kingdoms not of this world and kingdoms *of* this world, here was a letter wrote by even our worldly-minded brother unto Brother Hawkyard. Judge, from hearing of it read, whether Brother Hawkyard was the faithful steward that the Lord had in His mind only t'other day, when in this very place He drew you the picter of the unfaithful one; for it was Him that done it, not me. Don't doubt that!

Brother Gimblet then groaned and bellowed his way through my composition, and subsequently through an hour. The service closed with a hymn, in which the brothers unanimously roared, and the sisters unanimously shrieked at me, that I by wiles of worldly gain was mocked, and they on waters of sweet love were rocked; that I with mammon struggled in the dark, while they were floating in a second ark.

I went out from all this with an aching heart and a weary spirit: not because I was quite so weak as to consider these narrow creatures interpreters of the Divine Majesty and Wisdom, but because I was weak enough to feel as though it were my hard fortune to be misrepresented and misunderstood, when I most tried to subdue any risings of mere worldliness within me, and when I most hoped that, by dint of trying earnestly, I had succeeded.

Seventh Chapter

M Y TIMIDITY AND MY OBSCURITY occasioned me to live a secluded life at college, and to be little known. No relative ever came to visit me, for I had no relative. No intimate friends broke in upon my studies, for I made no intimate friends. I supported myself on my scholarship, and read much. My college time was otherwise not so very different from my time at Hoghton Towers.

Knowing myself to be unfit for the noisier stir of social existence, but believing myself qualified to do my duty in a moderate, though earnest way, if I could obtain some small preferment in the Church, I applied my mind to the clerical profession. In due sequence I took orders, was ordained and began to look about me for employment. I must observe that I had taken a good degree, that I had succeeded in winning a good fellowship, and that my means were ample for my retired way of life. By this time I had read with several young men; and the occupation increased my income, while it was highly interesting to me. I once accidentally overheard our greatest don say, to my boundless joy, "That he heard it reported of Silverman that his gift of quiet explanation, his patience, his amiable temper and his conscientiousness made him the best of coaches." May my "gift of quiet explanation" come more seasonably and powerfully to my aid in this present explanation than I think it will!

It may be in a certain degree owing to the situation of my college rooms (in a corner where the daylight was sobered), but it is in a much larger degree referable to the state of my own mind, that I seem to myself, on looking back to this time of my life, to have been always in the peaceful shade. I can see others in the sunlight; I can see our boats' crews and our athletic young men on the glistening water, or speckled with the moving lights of sunlit leaves; but I myself am always in the shadow looking on. Not unsympathetically – God forbid! – but looking on alone, much as I looked at Sylvia from the shadows of the ruined house, or looked at the red gleam shining through the farmer's windows, and listened to the fall of dancing feet, when all the ruin was dark that night in the quadrangle.

I now come to the reason of my quoting that laudation of myself above given. Without such reason, to repeat it would have been mere boastfulness.

Among those who had read with me was Mr Fareway, second son of Lady Fareway, widow of Sir Gaston Fareway, baronet. This young gentleman's abilities were much above the average; but he came of a rich family, and was idle and luxurious. He presented himself to me too late, and afterwards came to me too irregularly, to admit of my being of much service to him. In the end, I considered it my duty to dissuade him from going up for an examination which he could never pass; and he left college without a degree. After his departure, Lady Fareway wrote to me, representing the justice of my returning half my fee, as I had been of so little use to her son. Within my knowledge a similar demand had not been made in any other case; and I most freely admit that the justice of it had not occurred to me until it was pointed out. But I at once perceived it, yielded to it and returned the money.

Mr Fareway had been gone two years or more, and I had forgotten him, when he one day walked into my rooms as I was sitting at my books.

Said he, after the usual salutations had passed, "Mr Silverman, my mother is in town here, at the hotel, and wishes me to present you to her."

I was not comfortable with strangers, and I dare say I betrayed that I was a little nervous or unwilling. "For," said he, without my having spoken, "I think the interview may tend to the advancement of your prospects."

It put me to the blush to think that I should be tempted by a worldly reason, and I rose immediately.

Said Mr Fareway, as we went along, "Are you a good hand at business?"

"I think not," said I.

Said Mr Fareway then, "My mother is."

"Truly?" said I.

"Yes: my mother is what is usually called a managing woman. Doesn't make a bad thing, for instance, even out of the spendthrift habits of my eldest brother abroad. In short, a managing woman. This is in confidence."

He had never spoken to me in confidence, and I was surprised by his doing so. I said I should respect his confidence, of course, and said no more on the delicate subject. We had but a little way to walk, and I was soon in his mother's company. He presented me, shook hands with me, and left us two (as he said) to business.

I saw in my Lady Fareway a handsome, well-preserved lady of somewhat large stature, with a steady glare in her great round dark eyes that embarrassed me.

Said my lady, "I have heard from my son, Mr Silverman, that you would be glad of some preferment in the Church."

I gave my lady to understand that was so.

"I don't know whether you are aware," my lady proceeded, "that we have a presentation to a living? I say *we* have; but, in point of fact, *I* have."

I gave my lady to understand that I had not been aware of this.

Said my lady, "So it is: indeed I have two presentations – one to two hundred a year, one to six. Both livings are in our county – North Devonshire – as you probably know. The first is vacant. Would you like it?"

What with my lady's eyes, and what with the suddenness of this proposed gift, I was much confused.

"I am sorry it is not the larger presentation," said my lady, rather coldly, "though I will not, Mr Silverman, pay you the bad compliment of supposing that *you* are, because that would be mercenary – and mercenary I am persuaded you are not."

Said I, with my utmost earnestness, "Thank you, Lady Fareway, thank you, thank you! I should be deeply hurt if I thought I bore the character."

"Naturally," said my lady. "Always detestable, but particularly in a clergyman. You have not said whether you will like the living?"

With apologies for my remissness or indistinctness, I assured my lady that I accepted it most readily and gratefully. I added that I hoped she would not estimate my appreciation of the generosity of her choice by any flow of words; for I was not a ready man in that respect when taken by surprise or touched at heart.

"The affair is concluded," said my lady, "concluded. You will find the duties very light, Mr Silverman. Charming house; charming little garden, orchard, and all that. You will be able to take pupils. By the by! No: I will return to the word afterwards. What was I going to mention, when it put me out?"

My lady stared at me, as if I knew. And I didn't know. And that perplexed me afresh.

Said my lady, after some consideration, "Oh, of course, how very dull of me! The last incumbent – least mercenary man I ever saw – in consideration of the duties being so light and the house so delicious, couldn't rest, he said, unless I permitted him to help me with my correspondence, accounts and various little things of that kind; nothing in themselves, but which it worries a lady to cope with. Would Mr Silverman also like to?… Or shall I?…"

I hastened to say that my poor help would be always at Her Ladyship's service.

"I am absolutely blessed," said my lady, casting up her eyes (and so taking them off me for one moment), "in having to do with gentlemen who cannot endure an approach to the idea of being mercenary!" She shivered at the word. "And now as to the pupil."

"The?..." I was quite at a loss.

"Mr Silverman, you have no idea what she is. She is," said my lady, laying her touch upon my coat sleeve, "I do verily believe, the most extraordinary girl in this world. Already knows more Greek and Latin than Lady Jane Grey.* And taught herself! Has not yet, remember, derived a moment's advantage from Mr Silverman's classical acquirements. To say nothing of mathematics, which she is bent upon becoming versed in, and in which (as I hear from my son and others) Mr Silverman's reputation is so deservedly high!"

Under my lady's eyes I must have lost the clue, I felt persuaded; and yet I did not know where I could have dropped it.

"Adelina," said my lady, "is my only daughter. If I did not feel quite convinced that I am not blinded by a mother's partiality; unless I was absolutely sure that when you know her, Mr Silverman, you will esteem it a high and unusual privilege to direct her studies – I should introduce a mercenary element into this conversation, and ask you on what terms—"

I entreated my lady to go no further. My lady saw that I was troubled, and did me the honour to comply with my request.

Eighth Chapter

EVERYTHING IN MENTAL ACQUISITION that her brother might have been, if he would, and everything in all gracious charms and admirable qualities that no one but herself could be – this was Adelina.

I will not expatiate upon her beauty; I will not expatiate upon her intelligence, her quickness of perception, her powers of memory, her sweet consideration, from the first moment, for the slow-paced tutor who ministered to her wonderful gifts. I was thirty then; I am over sixty now: she is ever present to me in these hours as she was in those, bright and beautiful and young, wise and fanciful and good.

When I discovered that I loved her, how can I say? In the first day? In the first week? In the first month? Impossible to trace. If I be (as I am) unable to represent to myself any previous period of my life as quite separable from her attracting power, how can I answer for this one detail?

Whensoever I made the discovery, it laid a heavy burden on me. And yet, comparing it with the far heavier burden that I afterwards took up, it does not seem to me now to have been very hard to bear. In the knowledge that I did love her, and that I should love her while my life lasted, and that I was ever to hide my secret deep in my own breast, and she was never to find it, there was a kind of sustaining joy or pride, or comfort, mingled with my pain.

But later on – say, a year later on – when I made another discovery, then indeed my suffering and my struggle were strong. That other discovery was...

35

These words will never see the light, if ever, until my heart is dust; until her bright spirit has returned to the regions of which, when imprisoned here, it surely retained some unusual glimpse of remembrance; until all the pulses that ever beat around us shall have long been quiet; until all the fruits of all the tiny victories and defeats achieved in our little breasts shall have withered away. That discovery was that she loved me.

She may have enhanced my knowledge, and loved me for that; she may have overvalued my discharge of duty to her, and loved me for that; she may have refined upon a playful compassion which she would sometimes show for what she called my want of wisdom, according to the light of the world's dark lanterns, and loved me for that; she may – she must – have confused the borrowed light of what I had only learnt with its brightness in its pure, original rays; but she loved me at that time, and she made me know it.

Pride of family and pride of wealth put me as far off from her in my lady's eyes as if I had been some domesticated creature of another kind. But they could not put me farther from her than I put myself when I set my merits against hers. More than that. They could not put me, by millions of fathoms, half so low beneath her as I put myself when in imagination I took advantage of her noble trustfulness, took the fortune that I knew she must possess in her own right and left her to find herself, in the zenith of her beauty and genius, bound to poor rusty, plodding me.

No! Worldliness should not enter here at any cost. If I had tried to keep it out of other ground, how much harder was I bound to try to keep it out from this sacred place!

But there was something daring in her broad, generous character that demanded at so delicate a crisis to be delicately and patiently addressed. After many and many a bitter night (oh, I found I could cry for reasons not purely physical at this pass of my life!) I took my course.

My lady had, in our first interview, unconsciously overstated the accommodation of my pretty house. There was room in it for only one pupil. He was a young gentleman near coming of age, very well connected, but what is called a poor relation. His parents were dead. The charges of his living and reading with me were defrayed by an uncle; and he and I were to do our utmost together for three years towards qualifying him to make his way. At this time he had entered into his second year with me. He was well-looking, clever, energetic, enthusiastic, bold; in the best sense of the term, a thorough young Anglo-Saxon.

I resolved to bring these two together.

Ninth Chapter

SAID I, ONE NIGHT, when I had conquered myself, "Mr Granville" – Mr Granville Wharton his name was – "I doubt if you have ever yet so much as seen Miss Fareway."

"Well, sir," returned he, laughing, "you see her so much yourself that you hardly leave another fellow a chance of seeing her."

"I am her tutor, you know," said I.

And there the subject dropped for that time. But I so contrived as that they should come together shortly afterwards. I had previously so contrived as to keep them asunder; for while I loved her – I mean before I had determined on my sacrifice – a lurking jealousy of Mr Granville lay within my unworthy breast.

It was quite an ordinary interview in the Fareway Park; but they talked easily together for some time: like takes to like, and they had many points of resemblance. Said Mr Granville to me, when he and I sat at our supper that night, "Miss Fareway is remarkably beautiful, sir, remarkably engaging. Don't you think so?"

"I think so," said I. And I stole a glance at him, and saw that he had reddened and was thoughtful. I remember it most vividly, because the mixed feeling of grave pleasure and acute pain that the slight circumstance caused me was the first of a long, long series of such mixed impressions under which my hair turned slowly grey.

I had not much need to feign to be subdued; but I counterfeited to be older than I was in all respects (Heaven knows! My heart being all too young the while), and feigned to be more of a recluse and bookworm than I had really become, and gradually set up more and more of a fatherly manner towards Adelina. Likewise I made my tuition less imaginative than before; separated myself from my poets and philosophers; was careful to present them in their own light, and me, their lowly servant, in my own shade.

Moreover, in the matter of apparel I was equally mindful; not that I had ever been dapper that way, but that I was slovenly now.

As I depressed myself with one hand, so did I labour to raise Mr Granville with the other; directing his attention to such subjects as I too well knew most interested her and fashioning him (do not deride or misconstrue the expression, unknown reader of this writing; for I have suffered!) into a greater resemblance to myself in my solitary one strong aspect. And gradually, gradually, as I saw him take more and more to these thrown-out lures of mine, then did I come to know better and better that love was drawing him on, and was drawing her from me.

So passed more than another year; every day a year in its number of my mixed impressions of grave pleasure and acute pain; and then these two, being of age and free to act legally for themselves, came before me hand in hand (my hair being now quite white), and entreated me that I would unite them together. "And indeed, dear tutor," said Adelina, "it is but consistent in you that you should do this thing for us, seeing that we should never have spoken together that first time but for you, and that but for you we could never have met so often afterwards." The whole of which was literally true, for I had availed myself of my many business attendances on, and conferences with, my lady, to take Mr Granville to the house and leave him in the outer room with Adelina.

I knew that my lady would object to such a marriage for her daughter, or to any marriage that was other than an exchange of her for stipulated lands, goods and moneys. But looking on the two, and seeing with full eyes that they were both young and beautiful; and knowing that they were alike in the tastes and acquirements that will outlive youth and beauty; and considering that Adelina had a fortune now, in her own keeping; and considering further that Mr Granville, though for the present poor, was of a good family that had never lived in a cellar in Preston; and believing that their love would endure, neither having any great discrepancy to find out in the other – I told them of my readiness to do this thing which Adelina asked of her dear tutor, and to send them forth, husband and wife, into the shining world with golden gates that awaited them.

It was on a summer morning that I rose before the sun to compose myself for the crowning of my work with this end; and my dwelling being near to the sea, I walked down to the rocks on the shore, in order that I might behold the sun in his majesty.

The tranquillity upon the deep, and on the firmament, the orderly withdrawal of the stars, the calm promise of coming day, the rosy suffusion of the sky and waters, the ineffable splendour that then burst forth, attuned my mind afresh after the discords of the night. Methought that all I looked on said to me, and that all I heard in the sea and in the air said to me, "Be comforted, mortal, that thy life is so short. Our preparation for what is to follow has endured, and shall endure, for unimaginable ages."

I married them. I knew that my hand was cold when I placed it on their hands clasped together; but the words with which I had to accompany the action I could say without faltering, and I was at peace.

They being well away from my house and from the place after our simple breakfast, the time was come when I must do what I had pledged myself to them that I would do – break the intelligence to my lady.

I went up to the house, and found my lady in her ordinary business room. She happened to have an unusual amount of commissions to entrust to me that day, and she had filled my hands with papers before I could originate a word.

"My lady," I then began, as I stood beside her table.

"Why, what's the matter?" she said quickly, looking up.

"Not much, I would fain hope, after you shall have prepared yourself, and considered a little."

"Prepared myself – and considered a little! You appear to have prepared *your*self but indifferently, anyhow, Mr Silverman." This mighty scornfully, as I experienced my usual embarrassment under her stare.

Said I, in self-extenuation once for all, "Lady Fareway, I have but to say for myself that I have tried to do my duty."

"For yourself?" repeated my lady. "Then there are others concerned, I see. Who are they?"

I was about to answer, when she made towards the bell with a dart that stopped me, and said, "Why, where is Adelina?"

"Forbear! Be calm, my lady. I married her this morning to Mr Granville Wharton."

She set her lips, looked more intently at me than ever, raised her right hand, and smote me hard upon the cheek.

"Give me back those papers! Give me back those papers!" She tore them out of my hands, and tossed them on her table. Then seating herself defiantly in her great chair, and folding her arms, she stabbed me to the heart with the unlooked-for reproach, "You worldly wretch!"

"Worldly?" I cried. "Worldly?"

"This, if you please" – she went on with supreme scorn, pointing me out as if there were someone there to see – "this, if you please, is the disinterested scholar, with not a design beyond his books! This, if you please, is the simple creature whom any one could overreach in a bargain! This, if you please, is Mr Silverman! Not of this world; not he! He has too much simplicity for this world's cunning. He has too much singleness of purpose to be a match for this world's double-dealing. What did he give you for it?"

"For what? And who?"

"How much," she asked, bending forward in her great chair, and insultingly tapping the fingers of her right hand on the palm of her left, "how much does Mr Granville Wharton pay you for getting him Adelina's money? What is the amount of your percentage upon Adelina's fortune? What were the terms of the agreement that you proposed to this boy when you, the Revd George Silverman, licensed to marry, engaged to put him in possession of this girl? You made good terms for yourself, whatever they were. He would stand a poor chance against your keenness."

Bewildered, horrified, stunned by this cruel perversion, I could not speak. But I trust that I looked innocent, being so.

"Listen to me, shrewd hypocrite," said my lady, whose anger increased as she gave it utterance. "Attend to my words, you cunning schemer, who have carried this plot through with such a practised double face that I have never suspected you. I had my projects for my daughter; projects for family connexion; projects for fortune. You have thwarted them, and overreached me; but I am not one to be thwarted and overreached without retaliation. Do you mean to hold this living another month?"

"Do you deem it possible, Lady Fareway, that I can hold it another hour, under your injurious words?"

"Is it resigned, then?"

"It was mentally resigned, my lady, some minutes ago."

"Don't equivocate, sir. *Is* it resigned?"

"Unconditionally and entirely – and I would that I had never, never come near it!"

"A cordial response from me to *that* wish, Mr Silverman! But take this with you, sir. If you had not resigned it, I would have had you deprived of it. And though you have resigned it, you will not get quit of me as easily as you think, for I will pursue you with this story. I will make this nefarious conspiracy of yours, for money, known. You have made money by it, but you have at the same time made an enemy by it. *You* will take good care that the money sticks to you; I will take good care that the enemy sticks to you."

Then said I finally, "Lady Fareway, I think my heart is broken. Until I came into this room just now, the possibility of such mean wickedness as you have imputed to me never dawned upon my thoughts. Your suspicions—"

"Suspicions! Pah!" said she indignantly. "Certainties."

"Your certainties, my lady, as you call them, your suspicions as I call them, are cruel, unjust, wholly devoid of foundation in fact. I can declare no more; except that I have not acted for my own profit or my own pleasure. I have not in this proceeding considered myself. Once again, I think my heart is broken. If I have unwittingly done any wrong with a righteous motive, that is some penalty to pay."

She received this with another and more indignant "Pah!" and I made my way out of her room (I think I felt my way out with my hands, although my eyes were open), almost suspecting that my voice had a repulsive sound, and that I was a repulsive object.

There was a great stir made, the bishop was appealed to, I received a severe reprimand and narrowly escaped suspension. For years a cloud hung over me, and my name was tarnished. But my heart did not break, if a broken heart involves death; for I lived through it.

They stood by me, Adelina and her husband, through it all. Those who had known me at college, and even most of those who had only known me there by reputation, stood by me too. Little by little, the belief widened that I was not capable of what was laid to my charge. At length I was presented to a college living in a sequestered place, and there I now pen my explanation. I pen it at my open window in the summertime, before me, lying in the churchyard, equal resting place for sound hearts, wounded hearts and broken hearts. I pen it for the relief of my own mind, not foreseeing whether or no it will ever have a reader.

Hunted Down

Chapter I

M OST OF US SEE some romances in life. In my capacity as chief manager of a life-assurance office, I think I have within the last thirty years seen more romances than the generality of men, however unpromising the opportunity may, at first sight, seem.

As I have retired, and live at my ease, I possess the means that I used to want, of considering what I have seen, at leisure. My experiences have a more remarkable aspect, so reviewed, than they had when they were in progress. I have come home from the play now, and can recall the scenes of the drama upon which the curtain has fallen, free from the glare, bewilderment and bustle of the theatre.

Let me recall one of these romances of the real world.

There is nothing truer than physiognomy, taken in connection with manner. The art of reading that book of which Eternal Wisdom obliges every human creature to present his or her own page with the individual character written on it is a difficult one, perhaps, and is little studied. It may require some natural aptitude, and it must require (for everything does) some patience and some pains. That these are not usually given to it – that numbers of people accept a few stock commonplace expressions of the face as the whole list of characteristics, and neither seek nor know the refinements that are truest – that you, for instance, give a great deal of time and attention to the reading of music, Greek, Latin, French, Italian, Hebrew, if you please, and do not qualify yourself to read the face of the master or mistress looking over your shoulder teaching it to you – I assume to be five hundred times more probable than improbable. Perhaps a little self-sufficiency may be at the bottom of this; facial expression requires no study from you, you think; it comes by nature to you to know enough about it, and you are not to be taken in.

I confess, for my part, that I *have* been taken in, over and over again. I have been taken in by acquaintances, and I have been taken in (of course) by friends; far oftener by friends than by any other class of persons. How came I to be so deceived? Had I quite misread their faces?

No. Believe me, my first impression of those people, founded on face and manner alone, was invariably true. My mistake was in suffering them to come nearer to me and explain themselves away.

Chapter II

THE PARTITION WHICH SEPARATED my own office from our general outer office in the City was of thick plate glass. I could see through it what passed in the outer office, without hearing a word. I had it put up in place of a wall that had been there for years – ever since the house was built. It is no matter whether I did or did not make the change in order that I might derive my first impression of strangers, who came to us on business, from their faces alone, without being influenced by anything they said. Enough to mention that I turned my glass partition to that account, and that a life-assurance office is at all times exposed to be practised upon by the most crafty and cruel of the human race.

It was through my glass partition that I first saw the gentleman whose story I am going to tell.

He had come in without my observing it, and had put his hat and umbrella on the broad counter, and was bending over it to take some papers from one of the clerks. He was about forty or so, dark, exceedingly well dressed in black – being in mourning – and the hand he extended with a polite air had a particularly well-fitting black-kid glove upon it. His hair, which was elaborately brushed and oiled, was parted straight up the middle, and he presented this parting to the clerk, exactly (to my thinking) as if he had said, in so many words: "You must take me, if you please, my friend, just as I show myself. Come straight up here, follow the gravel path, keep off the grass, I allow no trespassing."

I conceived a very great aversion to that man the moment I thus saw him.

He had asked for some of our printed forms, and the clerk was giving them to him and explaining them. An obliged and agreeable smile was on his face, and his eyes met those of the clerk with a sprightly look. (I have known a vast quantity of nonsense talked about bad men not looking you in the face. Don't trust that conventional idea. Dishonesty will stare honesty out of countenance, any day in the week, if there is anything to be got by it.)

I saw, in the corner of his eyelash, that he became aware of my looking at him. Immediately he turned the parting in his hair towards the glass partition, as if he said to me with a sweet smile, "Straight up here, if you please. Off the grass!"

In a few moments he had put on his hat and taken up his umbrella, and was gone.

I beckoned the clerk into my room, and asked, "Who was that?"

He had the gentleman's card in his hand. "Mr Julius Slinkton, Middle Temple."

"A barrister, Mr Adams?"

"I think not, sir."

"I should have thought him a clergyman, but for his having no Reverend here," said I.

"Probably, from his appearance," Mr Adams replied, "he is reading for orders."

I should mention that he wore a dainty white cravat, and dainty linen altogether.

"What did he want, Mr Adams?"

"Merely a form of proposal, sir, and form of reference."

"Recommended here? Did he say?"

"Yes, he said he was recommended here by a friend of yours. He noticed you, but said that as he had not the pleasure of your personal acquaintance he would not trouble you."

"Did he know my name?"

"O yes, sir! He said, 'There *is* Mr Sampson, I see!'"

"A well-spoken gentleman, apparently?"

"Remarkably so, sir."

"Insinuating manners, apparently?"

"Very much so, indeed, sir."

"Hah!" said I. "I want nothing at present, Mr Adams."

Within a fortnight of that day I went to dine with a friend of mine, a merchant, a man of taste, who buys pictures and books, and the first man I saw among the company was Mr Julius Slinkton. There he was, standing before the fire, with good large eyes and an open expression of face; but still (I thought) requiring everybody to come at him by the prepared way he offered, and by no other.

I noticed him ask my friend to introduce him to Mr Sampson, and my friend did so. Mr Slinkton was very happy to see me. Not too happy; there was no overdoing of the matter; happy in a thoroughly well-bred, perfectly unmeaning way.

"I thought you had met," our host observed.

"No," said Mr Slinkton. "I did look in at Mr Sampson's office, on your recommendation; but I really did not feel justified in troubling Mr Sampson himself, on a point in the everyday routine of an ordinary clerk."

I said I should have been glad to show him any attention on our friend's introduction.

"I am sure of that," said he, "and am much obliged. At another time, perhaps, I may be less delicate. Only, however, if I have real business; for I know, Mr Sampson, how precious business time is, and what a vast number of impertinent people there are in the world."

I acknowledged his consideration with a slight bow. "You were thinking," said I, "of effecting a policy on your life."

"Oh dear no! I am afraid I am not so prudent as you pay me the compliment of supposing me to be, Mr Sampson. I merely enquired for a friend. But you know what friends are in such matters. Nothing may ever come of it. I have the greatest reluctance to trouble men of business with enquiries for friends, knowing the probabilities to be a thousand to one that the friends will never follow them up. People are so fickle, so selfish, so inconsiderate. Don't you, in your business, find them so every day, Mr Sampson?"

I was going to give a qualified answer, but he turned his smooth, white parting on me with its "Straight up here, if you please!" and I answered, "Yes."

"I hear, Mr Sampson," he resumed presently, for our friend had a new cook, and dinner was not so punctual as usual, "that your profession has recently suffered a great loss."

"In money?" said I.

He laughed at my ready association of loss with money, and replied, "No, in talent and vigour."

Not at once following out his allusion, I considered for a moment. "*Has* it sustained a loss of that kind?" said I. "I was not aware of it."

"Understand me, Mr Sampson. I don't imagine that you have retired. It is not so bad as that. But Mr Meltham—"

"Oh, to be sure!" said I. "Yes! Mr Meltham, the young actuary of the 'Inestimable'."

"Just so," he returned in a consoling way.

"He is a great loss. He was at once the most profound, the most original and the most energetic man I have ever known connected with life assurance."

I spoke strongly; for I had a high esteem and admiration for Meltham; and my gentleman had indefinitely conveyed to me some suspicion that he wanted to sneer at him. He recalled me to my guard by presenting that trim pathway up his head, with its infernal "Not on the grass, if you please – the gravel".

"You knew him, Mr Slinkton."

"Only by reputation. To have known him as an acquaintance or as a friend is an honour I should have sought if he had remained in society, though I might never have had the good fortune to attain it, being a man of far inferior mark. He was scarcely above thirty, I suppose?"

"About thirty."

"Ah!" he sighed in his former, consoling way. "What creatures we are! To break up, Mr Sampson, and become incapable of business at that time of life! Any reason assigned for the melancholy fact?"

("Humph!" thought I, as I looked at him. "But I won't go up the track, and I will go on the grass.")

"What reason have you heard assigned, Mr Slinkton?" I asked, point-blank.

"Most likely a false one. You know what Rumour is, Mr Sampson. I never repeat what I hear; it is the only way of paring the nails and shaving the head of Rumour. But when *you* ask me what reason I have heard assigned for Mr Meltham's passing away from among men, it is another thing. I am not gratifying idle gossip then. I was told, Mr Sampson, that Mr Meltham had relinquished all his avocations and all his prospects, because he was, in fact, broken-hearted. A disappointed attachment I heard – though it hardly seems probable, in the case of a man so distinguished and so attractive."

"Attractions and distinctions are no armour against death," said I.

"Oh, she died? Pray, pardon me. I did not hear that. That, indeed, makes it very, very sad. Poor Mr Meltham! She died? Ah, dear me! Lamentable, lamentable!"

I still thought his pity was not quite genuine, and I still suspected an unaccountable sneer under all this, until he said, as we were parted, like the other knots of talkers, by the announcement of dinner:

"Mr Sampson, you are surprised to see me so moved on behalf of a man whom I have never known. I am not so disinterested as you may suppose. I have suffered, and recently too, from death myself. I have lost one of two charming nieces, who were my constant companions. She died young – barely three-and-twenty; and even her remaining sister is far from strong. The world is a grave!"

He said this with deep feeling, and I felt reproached for the coldness of my manner. Coldness and distrust had been engendered in me, I knew, by my bad experiences; they were not natural to me; and I often thought how much I had lost in life, losing trustfulness, and how little I had gained, gaining hard caution. This state of mind being habitual to me, I troubled myself more about this conversation than I might have troubled myself about a greater matter. I listened to his talk at dinner, and observed how readily other men responded to it, and with what a graceful instinct he adapted his subjects to the knowledge and habits of those he talked with. As, in talking with me, he had easily started the subject I might be supposed to understand best, and to be the most interested in, so, in talking with others, he guided himself by the same rule. The company was of a varied character; but he was not at fault, that I could discover, with any member of it. He knew just as much of each man's pursuit as made him agreeable to that man in reference to it, and just as little as made it natural in him to seek modestly for information when the theme was broached.

As he talked and talked – but really not too much, for the rest of us seemed to force it upon him – I became quite angry with myself. I took his face to pieces in my mind, like a watch, and examined it in detail. I could not say much against any of his features separately; I could say even less against them when they were put together. "Then is it not monstrous," I asked myself, "that because a man happens to part his hair straight up the middle of his head, I should permit myself to suspect, and even to detest him?"

(I may stop to remark that this was no proof of my sense. An observer of men who finds himself steadily repelled by some apparently trifling thing in a stranger is right to give it great weight. It may be the clue to the whole mystery. A hair or two will show where a lion is hidden. A very little key will open a very heavy door.)

I took my part in the conversation with him after a time, and we got on remarkably well. In the drawing room I asked the host how long he had known Mr Slinkton. He answered, not many months; he had met him at the house of a celebrated painter then present, who had known him well when he was travelling with his nieces in Italy for their health. His plans in life being broken by the death of one of them, he was reading with the intention of going back to college as a matter of form, taking his degree and going into orders. I could not but argue with myself that here was the true explanation of his interest in poor Meltham, and that I had been almost brutal in my distrust on that simple head.

Chapter III

ON THE VERY NEXT DAY BUT ONE, I was sitting behind my glass partition, as before, when he came into the outer office, as before. The moment I saw him again without hearing him, I hated him worse than ever.

It was only for a moment that I had this opportunity; for he waved his tight-fitting black glove the instant I looked at him, and came straight in.

"Mr Sampson, good day! I presume, you see, upon your kind permission to intrude upon you. I don't keep my word in being justified by business, for my business here – if I may so abuse the word – is of the slightest nature."

I asked, was it anything I could assist him in?

"I thank you, no. I merely called to enquire outside whether my dilatory friend had been so false to himself as to be practical and sensible. But, of course, he has done nothing. I gave him your papers with my own hand, and he was hot upon the intention, but of course he has done nothing. Apart from the general human disinclination to do anything that ought to be done, I dare say there is a specialty about assuring one's life. You find it like will-making. People are so superstitious, and take it for granted they will die soon afterwards."

"Up here, if you please; straight up here, Mr Sampson. Neither to the right nor to the left." I almost fancied I could hear him breathe the words as he sat smiling at me, with that intolerable parting exactly opposite the bridge of my nose.

"There is such a feeling sometimes, no doubt," I replied, "but I don't think it obtains to any great extent."

"Well," said he, with a shrug and a smile, "I wish some good angel would influence my friend in the right direction. I rashly promised his mother and sister in Norfolk to see it done, and he promised them that he would do it. But I suppose he never will."

He spoke for a minute or two on indifferent topics, and went away.

I had scarcely unlocked the drawers of my writing table next morning, when he reappeared. I noticed that he came straight to the door in the glass partition, and did not pause a single moment outside.

"Can you spare me two minutes, my dear Mr Sampson?"

"By all means."

"Much obliged," laying his hat and umbrella on the table, "I came early, not to interrupt you. The fact is, I am taken by surprise in reference to this proposal my friend has made."

"Has he made one?" said I.

"Ye-es," he answered, deliberately looking at me; and then a bright idea seemed to strike him – "or he only tells me he has. Perhaps that may be a new way of evading the matter. By Jupiter, I never thought of that!"

Mr Adams was opening the morning's letters in the outer office. "What is the name, Mr Slinkton?" I asked.

"Beckwith."

I looked out at the door and requested Mr Adams, if there were a proposal in that name, to bring it in. He had already laid it out of his hand on the counter. It was easily selected from the rest, and he gave it me. Alfred Beckwith. Proposal to effect a policy with us for two thousand pounds. Dated yesterday.

"From the Middle Temple, I see, Mr Slinkton."

"Yes. He lives on the same staircase with me; his door is opposite. I never thought he would make me his reference though."

"It seems natural enough that he should."

"Quite so, Mr Sampson; but I never thought of it. Let me see." He took the printed paper from his pocket. "How am I to answer all these questions?"

"According to the truth, of course," said I.

"Oh, of course!" he answered, looking up from the paper with a smile. "I meant they were so many. But you do right to be particular. It stands to reason that you must be particular. Will you allow me to use your pen and ink?"

"Certainly."

"And your desk?"

"Certainly."

He had been hovering about between his hat and his umbrella for a place to write on. He now sat down in my chair, at my blotting paper and inkstand, with the long walk up his head in accurate perspective before me, as I stood with my back to the fire.

Before answering each question he ran over it aloud, and discussed it. How long had he known Mr Alfred Beckwith? That he had to calculate by years upon his fingers. What were his habits? No difficulty about them; temperate in the last degree, and took a little too much exercise, if anything. All the answers were satisfactory. When he had written them all, he looked them over, and finally signed them in a very pretty hand. He supposed he had now done with the business. I told him he was not likely to be troubled any further. Should he leave the papers there? If he pleased. Much obliged. Good morning.

I had had one other visitor before him; not at the office, but at my own house. That visitor had come to my bedside when it was not yet daylight, and had been seen by no one else but by my faithful confidential servant.

A second reference paper (for we required always two) was sent down into Norfolk, and was duly received back by post. This, likewise, was satisfactorily answered in every respect. Our forms were all complied with; we accepted the proposal, and the premium for one year was paid.

Chapter IV

FOR SIX OR SEVEN MONTHS I saw no more of Mr Slinkton. He called once at my house, but I was not at home; and he once asked me to dine with him in the Temple, but I was engaged. His friend's assurance was effected in March. Late in September or early in October I was down at Scarborough for a breath of sea air, where I met him on the beach. It was a hot evening; he came towards me with his hat in his hand; and there was the walk I had felt so strongly disinclined to take in perfect order again, exactly in front of the bridge of my nose.

He was not alone, but had a young lady on his arm.

She was dressed in mourning, and I looked at her with great interest. She had the appearance of being extremely delicate, and her face was remarkably pale and melancholy; but she was very pretty. He introduced her as his niece, Miss Niner.

"Are you strolling, Mr Sampson? Is it possible you can be idle?"

It *was* possible, and I *was* strolling.

"Shall we stroll together?"

"With pleasure."

The young lady walked between us, and we walked on the cool sea sand, in the direction of Filey.

"There have been wheels here," said Mr Slinkton. "And now I look again, the wheels of a hand carriage! Margaret, my love, your shadow without doubt!"

"Miss Niner's shadow?" I repeated, looking down at it on the sand.

"Not that one," Mr Slinkton returned, laughing. "Margaret, my dear, tell Mr Sampson."

"Indeed," said the young lady, turning to me, "there is nothing to tell – except that I constantly see the same invalid old gentleman at all times, wherever I go. I have mentioned it to my uncle, and he calls the gentleman my shadow."

"Does he live in Scarborough?" I asked.

"He is staying here."

"Do you live in Scarborough?"

"No, I am staying here. My uncle has placed me with a family here, for my health."

"And your shadow?" said I, smiling.

"My shadow," she answered, smiling too, "is – like myself – not very robust, I fear; for I lose my shadow sometimes, as my shadow loses me at other times. We both seem liable to confinement to the house. I have not seen my shadow for days and days; but it does oddly happen, occasionally, that wherever I go, for many days together, this gentleman goes. We have come together in the most unfrequented nooks on this shore."

"Is this he?" said I, pointing before us.

The wheels had swept down to the water's edge, and described a great loop on the sand in turning. Bringing the loop back towards us, and spinning it out as it came, was a hand carriage, drawn by a man.

"Yes," said Miss Niner, "this really is my shadow, uncle."

As the carriage approached us and we approached the carriage, I saw within it an old man, whose head was sunk on his breast, and who was enveloped in a variety of wrappers. He was drawn by a very quiet but very keen-looking man, with iron-grey hair, who was slightly lame. They had passed us, when the carriage stopped, and the old gentleman within, putting out his arm, called to me by my name. I went back, and was absent from Mr Slinkton and his niece for about five minutes.

When I rejoined them, Mr Slinkton was the first to speak. Indeed, he said to me in a raised voice before I came up with him:

"It is well you have not been longer, or my niece might have died of curiosity to know who her shadow is, Mr Sampson."

"An old East India Director," said I. "An intimate friend of our friend's, at whose house I first had the pleasure of meeting you. A certain Major Banks. You have heard of him?"

"Never."

"Very rich, Miss Niner; but very old, and very crippled. An amiable man, sensible – much interested in you. He has just been expatiating on the affection that he has observed to exist between you and your uncle."

Mr Slinkton was holding his hat again, and he passed his hand up the straight walk, as if he himself went up it serenely, after me.

"Mr Sampson," he said, tenderly pressing his niece's arm in his, "our affection was always a strong one, for we have had but few near ties. We have still fewer now. We have associations to bring us together that are not of this world, Margaret."

"Dear uncle!" murmured the young lady, and turned her face aside to hide her tears.

"My niece and I have such remembrances and regrets in common, Mr Sampson," he feelingly pursued, "that it would be strange indeed if the relations between us were cold or indifferent. If I remember a conversation we once had together, you will understand the reference I make. Cheer up, dear Margaret. Don't droop, don't droop. My Margaret! I cannot bear to see you droop!"

The poor young lady was very much affected, but controlled herself. His feelings, too, were very acute. In a word, he found himself under such great need of a restorative that he presently went away, to take a bath of seawater, leaving the young lady and me sitting by a point of rock, and probably presuming – but that you will say was a pardonable indulgence in a luxury – that she would praise him with all her heart.

She did, poor thing! With all her confiding heart, she praised him to me, for his care of her dead sister, and for his untiring devotion in her last illness. The sister had wasted away very slowly, and wild and terrible fantasies had come over her towards the end, but he had never been impatient with her, or at a loss; had always been gentle, watchful and self-possessed. The sister had known him, as she had known him, to be the best of men, the kindest of men, and yet a man of such admirable strength of character, as to be a very tower for the support of their weak natures while their poor lives endured.

"I shall leave him, Mr Sampson, very soon," said the young lady. "I know my life is drawing to an end; and when I am gone, I hope he will marry and be happy. I am sure he has lived single so long, only for my sake, and for my poor, poor sister's."

The little hand carriage had made another great loop on the damp sand, and was coming back again, gradually spinning out a slim figure of eight, half a mile long.

"Young lady," said I, looking around, laying my hand upon her arm, and speaking in a low voice, "time presses. You hear the gentle murmur of that sea?"

She looked at me with the utmost wonder and alarm, saying, "Yes!"

"And you know what a voice is in it when the storm comes?"

"Yes!"

"You see how quiet and peaceful it lies before us, and you know what an awful sight of power without pity it might be, this very night!"

"Yes!"

"But if you had never heard or seen it, or heard of it in its cruelty, could you believe that it beats every inanimate thing in its way to pieces, without mercy, and destroys life without remorse?"

"You terrify me, sir, by these questions!"

"To save you, young lady, to save you! For God's sake, collect your strength and collect your firmness! If you were here alone, and hemmed in by the rising tide on the flow to fifty feet above your head, you could not be in greater danger than the danger you are now to be saved from."

The figure on the sand was spun out, and straggled off into a crooked little jerk that ended at the cliff very near us.

"As I am, before Heaven and the Judge of all mankind, your friend, and your dead sister's friend, I solemnly entreat you, Miss Niner, without one moment's loss of time, to come to this gentleman with me!"

If the little carriage had been less near to us, I doubt if I could have got her away; but it was so near that we were there before she had recovered the hurry of being urged from the rock. I did not remain there with her two minutes. Certainly within five, I had the inexpressible satisfaction of seeing her – from the point we had sat on, and to which I had returned – half supported and half carried up some rude steps notched in the cliff, by the figure of an active man. With that figure beside her, I knew she was safe anywhere.

I sat alone on the rock, awaiting Mr Slinkton's return. The twilight was deepening and the shadows were heavy, when he came round the point, with his hat hanging at his buttonhole, smoothing his wet hair with one of his hands, and picking out the old path with the other and a pocket comb.

"My niece not here, Mr Sampson?" he said, looking about.

"Miss Niner seemed to feel a chill in the air after the sun was down, and has gone home."

He looked surprised, as though she were not accustomed to do anything without him; even to originate so slight a proceeding.

"I persuaded Miss Niner," I explained.

"Ah!" said he. "She is easily persuaded – for her good. Thank you, Mr Sampson; she is better within doors. The bathing place was farther than I thought, to say the truth."

"Miss Niner is very delicate," I observed.

He shook his head and drew a deep sigh. "Very, very, very. You may recollect my saying so. The time that has since intervened has not strengthened her. The gloomy shadow that fell upon her sister so early in life seems, in my anxious eyes, to gather over her, ever darker, ever darker. Dear Margaret, dear Margaret! But we must hope."

The hand carriage was spinning away before us at a most indecorous pace for an invalid vehicle, and was making most irregular curves upon the sand. Mr Slinkton, noticing it after he had put his handkerchief to his eyes, said:

"If I may judge from appearances, your friend will be upset, Mr Sampson."

"It looks probable, certainly," said I.

"The servant must be drunk."

"The servants of old gentlemen will get drunk sometimes," said I.

"The major draws very light, Mr Sampson."

"The major does draw light," said I.

By this time the carriage, much to my relief, was lost in the darkness. We walked on for a little, side by side over the sand, in silence. After a short while he said, in a voice still affected by the emotion that his niece's state of health had awakened in him, "Do you stay here long, Mr Sampson?"

"Why, no. I am going away tonight."

"So soon? But business always holds you in request. Men like Mr Sampson are too important to others to be spared to their own need of relaxation and enjoyment."

"I don't know about that," said I. "However, I am going back."

"To London?"

"To London."

"I shall be there too, soon after you."

I knew that as well as he did. But I did not tell him so. Any more than I told him what defensive weapon my right hand rested on in my pocket, as I walked by his side. Any more than I told him why I did not walk on the sea side of him with the night closing in.

We left the beach, and our ways diverged. We exchanged good-night, and had parted indeed, when he said, returning, "Mr

Sampson, *may* I ask? Poor Meltham, whom we spoke of – dead yet?"

"Not when I last heard of him; but too broken a man to live long, and hopelessly lost to his old calling."

"Dear, dear, dear!" said he, with great feeling. "Sad, sad, sad! The world is a grave!" And so went his way.

It was not his fault if the world were not a grave; but I did not call that observation after him, any more than I had mentioned those other things just now enumerated. He went his way, and I went mine with all expedition. This happened, as I have said, either at the end of September or beginning of October. The next time I saw him, and the last time, was late in November.

Chapter V

I HAD A VERY PARTICULAR ENGAGEMENT to breakfast in the Temple. It was a bitter north-easterly morning, and the sleet and slush lay inches deep in the streets. I could get no conveyance, and was soon wet to the knees; but I should have been true to that appointment, though I had to wade to it up to my neck in the same impediments.

The appointment took me to some chambers in the Temple. They were at the top of a lonely corner house overlooking the river. The name, MR ALFRED BECKWITH, was painted on the outer door. On the door opposite, on the same landing, the name MR JULIUS SLINKTON.

The doors of both sets of chambers stood open, so that anything said aloud in one set could be heard in the other.

I had never been in those chambers before. They were dismal, close, unwholesome and oppressive; the furniture, originally good, and not yet old, was faded and dirty – the rooms were in great disorder; there was a strong prevailing smell of opium, brandy and tobacco; the grate and fire irons were splashed all over with unsightly blotches of rust; and on a sofa by the fire, in the room where breakfast had been prepared, lay the host, Mr Beckwith, a man with all the appearances of the worst kind of drunkard, very far advanced upon his shameful way to death.

"Slinkton is not come yet," said this creature, staggering up when I went in. "I'll call him. Halloa! Julius Caesar! Come and drink!" As he hoarsely roared this out, he beat the poker and tongs together in a mad way, as if that were his usual manner of summoning his associate.

The voice of Mr Slinkton was heard through the clatter from the opposite side of the staircase, and he came in. He had not expected the pleasure of meeting me. I have seen several artful men brought to a stand, but I never saw a man so aghast as he was when his eyes rested on mine.

"Julius Caesar," cried Beckwith, staggering between us, "Mist' Sampson! Mist' Sampson, Julius Caesar! Julius, Mist' Sampson, is the friend of my soul. Julius keeps me plied with liquor, morning, noon and night. Julius is a real benefactor. Julius threw the tea and coffee out of window when I used to have any. Julius empties all the water jugs of their contents, and fills 'em with spirits. Julius winds me up and keeps me going. Boil the brandy, Julius!"

There was a rusty and furred saucepan in the ashes – the ashes looked like the accumulation of weeks – and Beckwith, rolling and staggering between us as if he were going to plunge headlong into the fire, got the saucepan out, and tried to force it into Slinkton's hand.

"Boil the brandy, Julius Caesar! Come! Do your usual office. Boil the brandy!"

He became so fierce in his gesticulations with the saucepan that I expected to see him lay open Slinkton's head with it. I therefore put out my hand to check him. He reeled back to the sofa, and sat there panting, shaking and red-eyed, in his rags of dressing gown, looking at us both. I noticed then that there was nothing to drink on the table but brandy, and nothing to eat but salted herrings, and a hot, sickly, highly peppered stew.

"At all events, Mr Sampson," said Slinkton, offering me the smooth gravel path for the last time, "I thank you for interfering between me and this unfortunate man's violence. However you came here, Mr Sampson, or with whatever motive you came here, at least I thank you for that."

"Boil the brandy," muttered Beckwith.

Without gratifying his desire to know how I came there, I said, quietly, "How is your niece, Mr Slinkton?"

He looked hard at me, and I looked hard at him.

"I am sorry to say, Mr Sampson, that my niece has proved treacherous and ungrateful to her best friend. She left me without a word of notice or explanation. She was misled, no doubt, by some designing rascal. Perhaps you may have heard of it."

"I did hear that she was misled by a designing rascal. In fact, I have proof of it."

"Are you sure of that?" said he.

"Quite."

"Boil the brandy," muttered Beckwith. "Company to breakfast, Julius Caesar. Do your usual office – provide the usual breakfast, dinner, tea and supper. Boil the brandy!"

The eyes of Slinkton looked from him to me, and he said, after a moment's consideration, "Mr Sampson, you are a man of the world, and so am I. I will be plain with you."

"O no, you won't," said I, shaking my head.

"I tell you, sir, I will be plain with you."

"And I tell you you will not," said I. "I know all about you. *You* plain with anyone? Nonsense, nonsense!"

"I plainly tell you, Mr Sampson, he went on, with a manner almost composed, "that I understand your object. You want to save your funds, and escape from your liabilities; these are old tricks of trade with you office gentlemen. But you will not do it, sir; you will not succeed. You have not an easy adversary to play against, when you play against me. We shall have to enquire, in due time, when and how Mr Beckwith fell into his present habits. With that remark, sir, I put this poor creature, and his incoherent wanderings of speech, aside, and wish you a good morning and a better case next time."

While he was saying this, Beckwith had filled a half-pint glass with brandy. At this moment, he threw the brandy at his face, and threw the glass after it. Slinkton put his hands up, half-blinded with the spirit, and cut with the glass across the forehead. At the sound of the breakage, a fourth person came into the room, closed the door and stood at it; he was a very quiet but very keen-looking man, with iron-grey hair and slightly lame.

Slinkton pulled out his handkerchief, assuaged the pain in his smarting eyes and dabbled the blood on his forehead. He was a long time about it, and I saw that in the doing of it a tremendous change came over him, occasioned by the change in Beckwith – who ceased to pant and tremble, sat upright and never took his eyes off him. I never in my life saw a face in which abhorrence and determination were so forcibly painted as in Beckwith's then.

"Look at me, you villain," said Beckwith, "and see me as I really am. I took these rooms, to make them a trap for you. I came into them as a drunkard, to bait the trap for you. You fell into the trap, and you will never leave it alive. On the morning when you last went to Mr Sampson's office, I had seen him first. Your plot has been known to both of us, all along, and you have been counter-plotted all along. What? Having been cajoled into putting that prize of two thousand pounds in your power, I was to be done to death with brandy, and, brandy not proving quick enough, with something quicker? Have I never seen you, when you thought my senses gone, pouring from your little bottle into my glass? Why, you murderer and forger, alone here with you in the dead of night,

72

as I have so often been, I have had my hand upon the trigger of a pistol, twenty times, to blow your brains out!"

This sudden starting-up of the thing that he had supposed to be his imbecile victim into a determined man, with a settled resolution to hunt him down and be the death of him, mercilessly expressed from head to foot, was, in the first shock, too much for him. Without any figure of speech, he staggered under it. But there is no greater mistake than to suppose that a man who is a calculating criminal is, in any phase of his guilt, otherwise than true to himself, and perfectly consistent with his whole character. Such a man commits murder, and murder is the natural culmination of his course; such a man has to outface murder, and will do it with hardihood and effrontery. It is a sort of fashion to express surprise that any notorious criminal, having such crime upon his conscience, can so brave it out. Do you think that if he had it on his conscience at all, or had a conscience to have it upon, he would ever have committed the crime?

Perfectly consistent with himself, as I believe all such monsters to be, this Slinkton recovered himself, and showed a defiance that was sufficiently cold and quiet. He was white, he was haggard, he was changed: but only as a sharper who had played for a great stake and had been outwitted and had lost the game.

"Listen to me, you villain," said Beckwith, "and let every word you hear me say be a stab in your wicked heart. When I took these rooms, to throw myself in your way and lead you on to the scheme that I knew my appearance and supposed character and habits would suggest to such a devil, how did I know that? Because you were no stranger to me. I knew you well. And I knew you to be the cruel wretch who, for so much money, had killed one innocent girl while she trusted him implicitly, and who was by inches killing another."

Slinkton took out a snuffbox, took a pinch of snuff, and laughed.

"But see here," said Beckwith, never looking away, never raising his voice, never relaxing his face, never unclenching his hand. "See what a dull wolf you have been, after all! The infatuated drunkard who never drank a fiftieth part of the liquor you plied him with, but poured it away, here, there, everywhere – almost before your eyes; who bought over the fellow you set to watch him and to ply him, by outbidding you in his bribe, before he had been at his work three days – with whom you have observed no caution, yet who was so bent on ridding the earth of you as a wild beast that he would have defeated you if you had been ever so prudent – that drunkard whom you have, many a time, left on the floor of this room, and who has even let you go out of it, alive and undeceived, when you have turned him over with your foot – has, almost as often, on the same night, within an hour, within a few minutes, watched you awake, had his hand at your pillow when you were asleep, turned over your papers, taken samples from your bottles and packets of powder, changed their contents, rifled every secret of your life!"

He had had another pinch of snuff in his hand, but had gradually let it drop from between his fingers to the floor; where he now smoothed it out with his foot, looking down at it the while.

"That drunkard," said Beckwith, "who had free access to your rooms at all times, that he might drink the strong drinks that you left in his way and be the sooner ended, holding no more terms with you than he would hold with a tiger, has had his master key for all your locks, his test for all your poisons, his clue to your cipher-writing. He can tell you, as well as you can tell him, how long it took to complete that deed, what doses there were, what intervals, what signs of gradual decay upon mind and body; what distempered fancies were produced, what observable changes, what physical pain. He can tell you, as well as you can tell him, that all this was recorded day by day, as a lesson of experience for future service. He can tell you, better than you can tell him, where that journal is at this moment."

Slinkton stopped the action of his foot, and looked at Beckwith.

"No," said the latter, as if answering a question from him. "Not in the drawer of the writing desk that opens with a spring; it is not there, and it never will be there again."

"Then you are a thief!" said Slinkton.

Without any change whatever in the inflexible purpose, which it was quite terrific even to me to contemplate, and from the power of which I had always felt convinced it was impossible for this wretch to escape, Beckwith returned, "And I am your niece's shadow, too."

With an imprecation Slinkton put his hand to his head, tore out some hair and flung it to the ground. It was the end of the smooth walk; he destroyed it in the action, and it will soon be seen that his use for it was past.

Beckwith went on: "Whenever you left here, I left here. Although I understood that you found it necessary to pause in the completion of that purpose, to avert suspicion, still I watched you close, with the poor confiding girl. When I had the diary, and could read it word by word – it was only about the night before your last visit to Scarborough – you remember the night? You slept with a small flat vial tied to your wrist – I sent to Mr Sampson, who was kept out of view. This is Mr Sampson's trusty servant standing by the door. We three saved your niece among us."

Slinkton looked at us all, took an uncertain step or two from the place where he had stood, returned to it, and glanced about him in a very curious way – as one of the meaner reptiles might, looking for a hole to hide in. I noticed at the same time that a singular change took place in the figure of the man – as if it collapsed within his clothes, and they consequently became ill-shapen and ill-fitting.

"You shall know," said Beckwith, "for I hope the knowledge will be bitter and terrible to you, why you have been pursued by one man, and why, when the whole interest that Mr Sampson represents would have expended any money in hunting you down, you have been tracked to death at a single individual's charge. I hear you have had the name of Meltham on your lips sometimes?"

I saw, in addition to those other changes, a sudden stoppage come upon his breathing.

"When you sent the sweet girl whom you murdered (you know with what artfully made-out surroundings and probabilities you sent her) to Meltham's office, before taking her abroad to originate the transaction that doomed her to the grave, it fell to Meltham's lot to see her and to speak with her. It did not fall to his lot to save her, though I know he would freely give his own life to have done it. He admired her – I would say he loved her deeply, if I thought it possible that you could understand the word. When she was sacrificed, he was thoroughly assured of your guilt. Having lost her, he had but one object left in life, and that was to avenge her and destroy you."

I saw the villain's nostrils rise and fall convulsively; but I saw no moving at his mouth.

"That man Meltham," Beckwith steadily pursued, "was as absolutely certain that you could never elude him in this world, if he devoted himself to your destruction with his utmost fidelity and earnestness, and if he divided the sacred duty with no other duty in life, as he was certain that in achieving it he would be a poor instrument in the hands of Providence, and would do well before Heaven in striking you out from among living men. I am that man, and I thank God that I have done my work!"

If Slinkton had been running for his life from swift-footed savages, a dozen miles, he could not have shown more emphatic signs of being oppressed at heart and labouring for breath, than he showed now, when he looked at the pursuer who had so relentlessly hunted him down.

"You never saw me under my right name before; you see me under my right name now. You shall see me once again in the body, when you are tried for your life. You shall see me once again in the spirit, when the cord is round your neck, and the crowd are crying against you!"

When Meltham had spoken these last words, the miscreant suddenly turned away his face, and seemed to strike his mouth with his open hand. At the same instant, the room was filled with a new and powerful odour and, almost at the same instant, he broke into a crooked run, leap, start – I have no name for the spasm – and fell, with a dull weight that shook the heavy old doors and windows in their frames.

That was the fitting end of him.

When we saw that he was dead, we drew away from the room, and Meltham, giving me his hand, said, with a weary air, "I have no more work on earth, my friend. But I shall see her again elsewhere."

It was in vain that I tried to rally him. He might have saved her, he said; he had not saved her, and he reproached himself; he had lost her, and he was broken-hearted.

"The purpose that sustained me is over, Sampson, and there is nothing now to hold me to life. I am not fit for life; I am weak and spiritless; I have no hope and no object; my day is done."

In truth, I could hardly have believed that the broken man who then spoke to me was the man who had so strongly and so differently impressed me when his purpose was before him. I used such entreaties with him, as I could; but he still said, and always said, in a patient, undemonstrative way – nothing could avail him – he was broken-hearted.

He died early in the next spring. He was buried by the side of the poor young lady for whom he had cherished those tender and unhappy regrets; and he left all he had to her sister. She lived to be a happy wife and mother; she married my sister's son, who succeeded poor Meltham; she is living now, and her children ride about the garden on my walking stick when I go to see her.

Holiday Romance

In Four Parts

Part I

T HIS BEGINNING PART is not made out of anybody's head,
you know. It's real. You must believe this beginning part
more than what comes after, else you won't understand how what
comes after came to be written. You must believe it all; but you
must believe this most, please. I am the editor of it. Bob Redforth
(he's my cousin, and shaking the table on purpose) wanted to be
the editor of it, but I said he shouldn't because he couldn't. *He*
has no idea of being an editor.

Nettie Ashford is my bride. We were married in the right-
hand closet in the corner of the dancing school, where first we
met, with a ring (a green one) from Wilkingwater's toy shop.
I owed for it out of my pocket money. When the rapturous
ceremony was over, we all four went up the lane and let off a
cannon (brought loaded in Bob Redforth's waistcoat pocket)
to announce our nuptials. It flew right up when it went off,
and turned over. Next day, Lieut. Col. Robin Redforth was
united, with similar ceremonies, to Alice Rainbird. This time
the cannon burst with a most terrific explosion, and made a
puppy bark.

My peerless bride was, at the period of which we now treat, in captivity at Miss Grimmer's. Drowvey and Grimmer is the partnership, and opinion is divided which is the greatest beast. The lovely bride of the colonel was also immured in the dungeons of the same establishment. A vow was entered into, between the colonel and myself, that we would cut them out on the following Wednesday when walking two and two.

Under the desperate circumstances of the case, the active brain of the colonel, combining with his lawless pursuit (he is a pirate), suggested an attack with fireworks. This, however, from motives of humanity, was abandoned as too expensive.

Lightly armed with a paper knife buttoned up under his jacket, and waving the dreaded black flag at the end of a cane, the colonel took command of me at two p.m. on the eventful and appointed day. He had drawn out the plan of attack on a piece of paper, which was rolled up round a hoop stick. He showed it to me. My position and my full-length portrait (but my real ears don't stick out horizontal) was behind a corner lamp-post, with written orders to remain there till I should see Miss Drowvey fall. The Drowvey who was to fall was the one in spectacles, not the one with the large lavender bonnet. At that signal I was to rush forth, seize my bride and fight my way to the lane. There a junction would be effected between myself and the colonel; and putting our brides behind us, between ourselves and the palings, we were to conquer or die.

The enemy appeared – approached. Waving his black flag, the colonel attacked. Confusion ensued. Anxiously I awaited my signal; but my signal came not. So far from falling, the hated Drowvey in spectacles appeared to me to have muffled the colonel's head in his outlawed banner, and to be pitching into him with a parasol. The one in the lavender bonnet also performed prodigies of valour with her fists on his back. Seeing that all was for the moment lost, I fought my desperate way hand to hand to the lane. Through taking the back road, I was so fortunate as to meet nobody, and arrived there uninterrupted.

It seemed an age ere the colonel joined me. He had been to the jobbing tailor's to be sewn up in several places, and attributed our defeat to the refusal of the detested Drowvey to fall. Finding her so obstinate, he had said to her "Die, recreant!" but had found her no more open to reason on that point than the other.

My blooming bride appeared, accompanied by the colonel's bride, at the dancing school next day. What? Was her face averted from me? Hah? Even so. With a look of scorn, she put into my hand a bit of paper, and took another partner. On the paper was pencilled, "Heavens! Can I write the word? Is my husband a cow?"

In the first bewilderment of my heated brain, I tried to think what slanderer could have traced my family to the ignoble animal mentioned above. Vain were my endeavours. At the end of that dance I whispered the colonel to come into the cloakroom, and I showed him the note.

"There is a syllable wanting," said he, with a gloomy brow.

"Hah! What syllable?" was my enquiry.

"She asks, can she write the word? And no; you see she couldn't," said the colonel, pointing out the passage.

"And the word was?" said I.

"Cow... cow... coward," hissed the pirate colonel in my ear, and gave me back the note.

Feeling that I must for ever tread the earth a branded boy – person I mean – or that I must clear up my honour, I demanded to be tried by a court-martial. The colonel admitted my right to be tried. Some difficulty was found in composing the court, on account of the Emperor of France's aunt refusing to let him come out. He was to be the president. Ere yet we had appointed a substitute, he made his escape over the back wall, and stood among us, a free monarch.

The court was held on the grass by the pond. I recognized, in a certain admiral among my judges, my deadliest foe. A coconut had given rise to language that I could not brook; but confiding in my innocence, and also in the knowledge that the President of the United States (who sat next him) owed me a knife, I braced myself for the ordeal.

It was a solemn spectacle, that court. Two executioners with pinafores reversed led me in. Under the shade of an umbrella I perceived my bride, supported by the bride of the pirate colonel. The president, having reproved a little female ensign for tittering, on a matter of life or death, called upon me to plead, "Coward or no coward, guilty or not guilty?" I pleaded in a firm tone, "No coward and not guilty." (The little female ensign being again reproved by the president for misconduct, mutinied, left the court and threw stones.)

My implacable enemy, the admiral, conducted the case against me. The colonel's bride was called to prove that I had remained behind the corner lamp-post during the engagement. I might have been spared the anguish of my own bride's being also made a witness to the same point, but the admiral knew where to wound me. Be still, my soul, no matter. The colonel was then brought forward with his evidence.

It was for this point that I had saved myself up, as the turning point of my case. Shaking myself free of my guards – who had no business to hold me, the stupids, unless I was found guilty – I asked the colonel what he considered the first duty of a soldier? Ere he could reply, the President of the United States rose and informed the court that my foe, the admiral, had suggested "Bravery", and that prompting a witness wasn't fair. The president of the court immediately ordered the admiral's mouth to be filled with leaves, and tied up with string. I had the satisfaction of seeing the sentence carried into effect before the proceedings went further.

I then took a paper from my trousers pocket, and asked, "What do you consider, Col. Redford, the first duty of a soldier? Is it obedience?"

"It is," said the colonel.

"Is that paper – please to look at it – in your hand?"

"It is," said the colonel.

"Is it a military sketch?"

"It is," said the colonel.

"Of an engagement?"

"Quite so," said the colonel.

"Of the late engagement?"

"Of the late engagement."

"Please to describe it, and then hand it to the president of the court."

From that triumphant moment my sufferings and my dangers were at an end. The court rose up and jumped, on discovering that I had strictly obeyed orders. My foe, the admiral, who though muzzled was malignant yet, contrived to suggest that I was dishonoured by having quitted the field. But the colonel himself had done as much, and gave his opinion, upon his word and honour as a pirate, that when all was lost the field might be quitted without disgrace. I was going to be found "No coward and not guilty", and my blooming bride was going to be publicly restored to my arms in a procession, when an unlooked-for event disturbed the general rejoicing. This was no other than the Emperor of France's aunt catching hold of his hair. The proceedings abruptly terminated, and the court tumultuously dissolved.

It was when the shades of the next evening but one were beginning to fall, ere yet the silver beams of Luna touched the earth, that four forms might have been descried slowly advancing towards the weeping willow on the borders of the pond, the now deserted scene of the day before yesterday's agonies and triumphs. On a nearer approach, and by a practised eye, these might have been identified as the forms of the pirate colonel with his bride, and of the day before yesterday's gallant prisoner with his bride.

On the beauteous faces of the nymphs dejection sat enthroned. All four reclined under the willow for some minutes without speaking, till at length the bride of the colonel poutingly observed, "It's of no use pretending any more, and we had better give it up."

"Hah!" exclaimed the pirate. "Pretending?"

"Don't go on like that; you worry me," returned his bride.

The lovely bride of Tinkling echoed the incredible declaration. The two warriors exchanged stony glances.

"If," said the bride of the pirate colonel, "grown-up people WON'T do what they ought to do, and WILL put us out, what comes of our pretending?"

"We only get into scrapes," said the bride of Tinkling.

"You know very well," pursued the colonel's bride, "that Miss Drowvey wouldn't fall. You complained of it yourself. And you know how disgracefully the court-martial ended. As to our marriage: would my people acknowledge it at home?"

"Or would my people acknowledge ours?" said the bride of Tinkling.

Again the two warriors exchanged stony glances.

"If you knocked at the door and claimed me, after you were told to go away," said the colonel's bride, "you would only have your hair pulled, or your ears, or your nose."

"If you persisted in ringing at the bell and claiming me," said the bride of Tinkling to that gentleman, "you would have things dropped on your head from the window over the handle, or you would be played upon by the garden engine."

"And at your own homes," resumed the bride of the colonel, "it would be just as bad. You would be sent to bed, or something equally undignified. Again, how would you support us?"

The pirate colonel replied in a courageous voice, "By rapine!" But his bride retorted, "Suppose the grown-up people wouldn't be rapined?"

"Then," said the colonel, "they should pay the penalty in blood."

"But suppose they should object," retorted his bride, "and wouldn't pay the penalty in blood or anything else?"

A mournful silence ensued.

"Then do you no longer love me, Alice?" asked the colonel.

"Redforth! I am ever thine," returned his bride.

"Then do you no longer love me, Nettie?" asked the present writer.

"Tinkling! I am ever thine," returned my bride.

We all four embraced. Let me not be misunderstood by the giddy. The colonel embraced his own bride, and I embraced mine. But two times two make four.

"Nettie and I," said Alice mournfully, "have been considering our position. The grown-up people are too strong for us. They make us ridiculous. Besides, they have changed the times. William Tinkling's baby brother was christened yesterday. What took place? Was any king present? Answer, William."

I said no, unless disguised as Great-Uncle Chopper.

"Any queen?"

There had been no queen that I knew of at our house. There might have been one in the kitchen: but I didn't think so, or the servants would have mentioned it.

"Any fairies?"

None that were visible.

"We had an idea among us, I think," said Alice, with a melancholy smile, "we four, that Miss Grimmer would prove to be the wicked fairy, and would come in at the christening with her crutch stick, and give the child a bad gift. Was there anything of that sort? Answer, William."

I said that Ma had said afterwards (and so she had), that Great-Uncle Chopper's gift was a shabby one; but she hadn't said a bad one. She had called it shabby, electrotyped, second-hand and below his income.

"It must be the grown-up people who have changed all this," said Alice. "*We* couldn't have changed it, if we had been so inclined, and we never should have been. Or perhaps Miss Grimmer *is* a wicked fairy after all, and won't act up to it because the grown-up people have persuaded her not to. Either way, they would make us ridiculous if we told them what we expected."

"Tyrants!" muttered the pirate colonel.

"Nay, my Redforth," said Alice, "say not so. Call not names, my Redforth, or they will apply to Pa."

"Let 'em," said the colonel. "I do not care. Who's he?"

89

Tinkling here undertook the perilous task of remonstrating with his lawless friend, who consented to withdraw the moody expressions above quoted.

"What remains for us to do?" Alice went on in her mild, wise way. "We must educate, we must pretend in a new manner, we must wait."

The colonel clenched his teeth – four out in front, and a piece of another, and he had been twice dragged to the door of a dentist despot, but had escaped from his guards. "How educate? How pretend in a new manner? How wait?"

"Educate the grown-up people," replied Alice. "We part tonight. Yes, Redforth" – for the colonel tucked up his cuffs – "part tonight! Let us in these next holidays, now going to begin, throw our thoughts into something educational for the grown-up people, hinting to them how things ought to be. Let us veil our meaning under a mask of romance; you, I and Nettie. William Tinkling, being the plainest and quickest writer, shall copy out. Is it agreed?"

The colonel answered sulkily, "I don't mind." He then asked, "How about pretending?"

"We will pretend," said Alice, "that we are children; not that we are those grown-up people who won't help us out as they ought, and who understand us so badly."

The colonel, still much dissatisfied, growled, "How about waiting?"

"We will wait," answered little Alice, taking Nettie's hand in hers, and looking up to the sky, "we will wait – ever constant and true – till the times have got so changed as that everything helps us out, and nothing makes us ridiculous, and the fairies have come back. We will wait – ever constant and true – till we are eighty, ninety or one hundred. And then the fairies will send *us* children, and we will help them out, poor pretty little creatures, if they pretend ever so much."

"So we will, dear," said Nettie Ashford, taking her round the waist with both arms and kissing her. "And now if my husband will go and buy some cherries for us, I have got some money."

In the friendliest manner I invited the colonel to go with me, but he so far forgot himself as to acknowledge the invitation by kicking out behind, and then lying down on his stomach on the grass, pulling it up and chewing it. When I came back, however, Alice had nearly brought him out of his vexation, and was soothing him by telling him how soon we should all be ninety.

As we sat under the willow tree and ate the cherries (fair, for Alice shared them out), we played at being ninety. Nettie complained that she had a bone in her old back, and it made her hobble; and Alice sang a song in an old woman's way, but it was very pretty, and we were all merry. At least, I don't know about merry exactly, but all comfortable.

There was a most tremendous lot of cherries; and Alice always had with her some neat little bag or box or case, to hold things. In it that night was a tiny wineglass. So Alice and Nettie said they would make some cherry wine to drink our love at parting.

Each of us had a glassful, and it was delicious; and each of us drank the toast, "Our love at parting". The colonel drank his wine last, and it got into my head directly that it got into his directly. Anyhow, his eyes rolled immediately after he had turned the glass upside down, and he took me on one side and proposed in a hoarse whisper, that we should "cut 'em out still".

"How did he mean?" I asked my lawless friend.

"Cut our brides out," said the colonel, "and then cut our way, without going down a single turning, bang to the Spanish main!"

We might have tried it, though I didn't think it would answer; only we looked round and saw that there was nothing but moonlight under the willow tree, and that our pretty, pretty wives were gone. We burst out crying. The colonel gave in second, and came to first; but he gave in strong.

We were ashamed of our red eyes, and hung about for half an hour to whiten them. Likewise a piece of chalk round the rims, I doing the colonel's, and he mine, but afterwards found in the bedroom looking glass not natural, besides inflammation. Our conversation turned on being ninety. The colonel told me he had a pair of boots that wanted soling and heeling; but he thought it hardly worthwhile to mention it to his father, as he himself should so soon be ninety, when he thought shoes would be more convenient. The colonel also told me, with his hand upon his hip, that he felt himself already getting on in life, and turning rheumatic. And I told him the same. And when they said at our house at supper (they are always bothering about something) that I stooped, I felt so glad!

This is the end of the beginning part that you were to believe most.

Part II

ROMANCE. FROM THE PEN
OF MISS ALICE RAINBIRD*

T HERE WAS ONCE A KING, and he had a queen; and he was the manliest of his sex, and she was the loveliest of hers. The King was, in his private profession, under government. The Queen's father had been a medical man out of town.

They had nineteen children, and were always having more. Seventeen of these children took care of the baby; and Alicia, the eldest, took care of them all. Their ages varied from seven years to seven months.

Let us now resume our story.

One day the King was going to the office, when he stopped at the fishmonger's to buy a pound and a half of salmon not too near the tail, which the Queen (who was a careful housekeeper) had requested him to send home. Mr Pickles, the fishmonger, said, "Certainly, sir; is there any other article? Good morning."

The King went on towards the office in a melancholy mood; for quarter-day* was such a long way off, and several of the dear children were growing out of their clothes. He had not proceeded far when Mr Pickles's errand boy came running after him and said, "Sir, you didn't notice the old lady in our shop."

"What old lady?" enquired the king. "I saw none."

Now the King had not seen any old lady, because this old lady had been invisible to him, though visible to Mr Pickles's boy. Probably because he messed and splashed the water about to that degree, and flopped the pairs of soles down in that violent manner, that, if she had not been visible to him, he would have spoilt her clothes.

Just then the old lady came trotting up. She was dressed in shot silk of the richest quality, smelling of dried lavender.

"King Watkins the First, I believe?" said the old lady.

"Watkins," replied the King, "is my name."

"Papa, if I am not mistaken, of the beautiful Princess Alicia?" said the old lady.

"And of eighteen other darlings," replied the King.

"Listen. You are going to the office," said the old lady.

It instantly flashed upon the King that she must be a fairy, or how could she know that?

"You are right," said the old lady, answering his thoughts. "I am the good Fairy Grandmarina. Attend! When you return home to dinner, politely invite the Princess Alicia to have some of the salmon you bought just now."

"It may disagree with her," said the King.

The old lady became so very angry at this absurd idea that the King was quite alarmed, and humbly begged her pardon.

"We hear a great deal too much about this thing disagreeing and that thing disagreeing," said the old lady, with the greatest contempt it was possible to express. "Don't be greedy. I think you want it all yourself."

The King hung his head under this reproof, and said he wouldn't talk about things disagreeing any more.

"Be good, then," said the Fairy Grandmarina, "and don't. When the beautiful Princess Alicia consents to partake of the salmon – as I think she will – you will find she will leave a fishbone on her plate. Tell her to dry it, and to rub it, and to polish it till it shines like mother-of-pearl, and to take care of it as a present from me."

"Is that all?" asked the King.

"Don't be impatient, sir," returned the fairy Grandmarina, scolding him severely. "Don't catch people short, before they have done speaking. Just the way with you grown-up persons. You are always doing it."

The King again hung his head, and said he wouldn't do so any more.

"Be good, then," said the Fairy Grandmarina, "and don't! Tell the Princess Alicia, with my love, that the fishbone is a magic present which can only be used once; but that it will bring her, that once, whatever she wishes for, PROVIDED SHE WISHES FOR IT AT THE RIGHT TIME. That is the message. Take care of it."

The King was beginning, "Might I ask the reason?" when the fairy became absolutely furious.

"*Will* you be good, sir?" she exclaimed, stamping her foot on the ground. "The reason for this, and the reason for that, indeed! You are always wanting the reason. No reason. There! Hoity toity me! I am sick of your grown-up reasons."

The King was extremely frightened by the old lady's flying into such a passion, and said he was very sorry to have offended her, and he wouldn't ask for reasons any more.

"Be good, then," said the old lady, "and don't!"

With those words, Grandmarina vanished, and the King went on and on and on, till he came to the office. There he wrote and wrote and wrote, till it was time to go home again. Then he politely invited the Princess Alicia, as the fairy had directed him, to partake of the salmon. And when she had enjoyed it very much, he saw the fishbone on her plate, as the fairy had told him he would, and he delivered the fairy's message, and the Princess Alicia took care to dry the bone, and to rub it, and to polish it, till it shone like mother-of-pearl.

And so, when the Queen was going to get up in the morning, she said, "Oh, dear me, dear me; my head, my head!" and then she fainted away.

The Princess Alicia, who happened to be looking in at the chamber door, asking about breakfast, was very much alarmed when she saw her royal mamma in this state, and she rang the bell for Peggy, which was the name of the lord chamberlain. But remembering where the smelling bottle was, she climbed on a chair and got it; and after that she climbed on another chair by the bedside, and held the smelling bottle to the Queen's nose; and after that she jumped down and got some water; and after that she jumped up again and wetted the queen's forehead; and, in short, when the lord chamberlain came in, that dear old woman said to the little princess, "What a trot you are! I couldn't have done it better myself!"

But that was not the worst of the good Queen's illness. Oh, no! She was very ill indeed, for a long time. The Princess Alicia kept the seventeen young princes and princesses quiet, and dressed and undressed and danced the baby, and made the kettle boil, and heated the soup, and swept the hearth, and poured out the medicine, and nursed the queen, and did all that ever she could, and was as busy, busy, busy as busy could be; for there were not many servants at that palace for three reasons: because the King was short of money, because a rise in his office never seemed to come, and because quarter-day was so far off that it looked almost as far off and as little as one of the stars.

But on the morning when the Queen fainted away, where was the magic fishbone? Why, there it was in the Princess Alicia's pocket! She had almost taken it out to bring the Queen to life again, when she put it back, and looked for the smelling bottle.

After the Queen had come out of her swoon that morning, and was dozing, the Princess Alicia hurried upstairs to tell a most particular secret to a most particularly confidential friend of hers, who was a duchess. People did suppose her to be a doll; but she was really a duchess, though nobody knew it except the princess.

This most particular secret was the secret about the magic fish-bone, the history of which was well known to the duchess, because the princess told her everything. The princess kneeled down by the bed on which the duchess was lying, full-dressed and wide awake, and whispered the secret to her. The duchess smiled and nodded. People might have supposed that she never smiled and nodded; but she often did, though nobody knew it except the princess.

Then the Princess Alicia hurried downstairs again, to keep watch in the Queen's room. She often kept watch by herself in the Queen's room; but every evening, while the illness lasted, she sat there watching with the King. And every evening the King sat looking at her with a cross look, wondering why she never brought out the magic fishbone. As often as she noticed this, she ran upstairs, whispered the secret to the duchess over again, and said to the duchess besides, "They think we children never have a reason or a meaning!" And the duchess, though the most fashionable duchess that ever was heard of, winked her eye.

"Alicia," said the King, one evening, when she wished him goodnight.

"Yes, Papa."

"What is become of the magic fishbone?"

"In my pocket, Papa!"

"I thought you had lost it?"

"Oh, no, Papa!"

"Or forgotten it?"

"No, indeed, Papa."

And so another time the dreadful little snapping pug dog next door made a rush at one of the young princes as he stood on the steps coming home from school, and terrified him out of his wits; and he put his hand through a pane of glass, and bled, bled, bled. When the seventeen other young princes and princesses saw him bleed, bleed, bleed, they were terrified out of their wits too, and screamed themselves black in their seventeen faces all at once. But the Princess Alicia put her hands over all their seventeen mouths, one after another, and persuaded them to be quiet because of the sick Queen. And then she put the wounded prince's hand in a basin of fresh cold water, while they stared with their – twice seventeen are thirty-four, put down four and carry three – eyes, and then she looked in the hand for bits of glass, and there were fortunately no bits of glass there. And then she said to two chubby-legged princes, who were sturdy though small, "Bring me in the royal ragbag: I must snip and stitch and cut and contrive." So these two young princes tugged at the royal ragbag, and lugged it in; and the Princess Alicia sat down on the floor, with a large pair of scissors and a needle and thread, and snipped and stitched and cut and contrived, and made a bandage, and put it on, and it fitted beautifully; and so when it was all done, she saw the King her papa looking on by the door.

"Alicia."

"Yes, Papa."

"What have you been doing?"

"Snipping, stitching, cutting and contriving, Papa."

"Where is the magic fishbone?"

"In my pocket, Papa."

"I thought you had lost it?"

"Oh, no, Papa."

"Or forgotten it?"

"No, indeed, Papa."

After that, she ran upstairs to the duchess, and told her what had passed, and told her the secret over again; and the duchess shook her flaxen curls, and laughed with her rosy lips.

Well! And so another time the baby fell under the grate. The seventeen young princes and princesses were used to it; for they were almost always falling under the grate or down the stairs; but the baby was not used to it yet, and it gave him a swelled face and a black eye. The way the poor little darling came to tumble was that he was out of the Princess Alicia's lap just as she was sitting, in a great coarse apron that quite smothered her, in front of the kitchen fire, beginning to peel the turnips for the broth for dinner; and the way she came to be doing that was that the King's cook had run away that morning with her own true love, who was a very tall but very tipsy soldier. Then the seventeen young princes and princesses, who cried at everything that happened, cried and roared. But the Princess Alicia (who couldn't help crying a little herself) quietly called to them to be still, on account of not throwing back the Queen upstairs, who was fast getting well, and said, "Hold your tongues, you wicked little monkeys, every one of you, while I examine Baby!" Then she examined Baby, and found that he hadn't broken anything; and she held cold iron to his poor dear eye, and smoothed his poor dear face, and he presently fell asleep in her arms. Then she said to the seventeen princes and princesses, "I am afraid to let him down yet, lest he should wake and feel pain; be good, and you shall all be cooks." They jumped for joy when they heard that, and began making themselves cooks' caps out of old newspapers. So to one she gave the saltbox, and to one she gave the barley, and to one she gave the herbs, and to one she gave the turnips, and to one she gave the carrots, and to one she gave the onions, and to one she gave the spice box, till they were all cooks, and all running about at work, she sitting in the middle, smothered in the great coarse apron, nursing Baby. By and by the broth was done; and the baby woke up, smiling like an angel, and was trusted to the sedatest princess to hold, while the other princes and princesses were squeezed into a far-off corner to look at the Princess Alicia turning out the saucepanful of broth, for fear (as they were always getting into trouble) they should get splashed and scalded. When the broth came tumbling out, steaming beautifully, and smelling like a nosegay good to eat, they clapped their hands. That made the baby clap his hands; and that, and his looking as if he had a comic toothache, made all the princes and princesses laugh. So the Princess Alicia said, "Laugh and be good; and after dinner we will make him a nest on the floor in a corner, and he shall sit in his nest and see a dance of eighteen cooks." That delighted the young princes and princesses, and they ate up all the broth, and washed up all the plates and dishes, and cleared away, and pushed the table into a corner; and then they in their cooks' caps, and the Princess Alicia in the smothering coarse apron that belonged to the cook that had run away with her own true love that was the very tall but very tipsy soldier, danced a dance of eighteen cooks before the angelic baby, who forgot his swelled face and his black eye and crowed with joy.

And so then, once more the Princess Alicia saw King Watkins the First, her father, standing in the doorway looking on, and he said, "What have you been doing, Alicia?"

"Cooking and contriving, Papa."

"What else have you been doing, Alicia?"

"Keeping the children light-hearted, Papa."

"Where is the magic fishbone, Alicia?"

"In my pocket, Papa."

"I thought you had lost it?"

"Oh, no, Papa!"

"Or forgotten it?"

"No, indeed, Papa."

The King then sighed so heavily, and seemed so low-spirited, and sat down so miserably, leaning his head upon his hand, and his elbow upon the kitchen table pushed away in the corner, that the seventeen princes and princesses crept softly out of the kitchen, and left him alone with the Princess Alicia and the angelic baby.

"What is the matter, Papa?"

"I am dreadfully poor, my child."

"Have you no money at all, Papa?"

"None, my child."

"Is there no way of getting any, Papa?"

"No way," said the King. "I have tried very hard, and I have tried all ways."

When she heard those last words, the Princess Alicia began to put her hand into the pocket where she kept the magic fishbone.

"Papa," said she, "when we have tried very hard, and tried all ways, we must have done our very, very best?"

"No doubt, Alicia."

"When we have done our very, very best, Papa, and that is not enough, then I think the right time must have come for asking help of others." This was the very secret connected with the magic fishbone, which she had found out for herself from the good Fairy Grandmarina's words, and which she had so often whispered to her beautiful and fashionable friend, the duchess.

So she took out of her pocket the magic fishbone, that had been dried and rubbed and polished till it shone like mother-of-pearl; and she gave it one little kiss, and wished it was quarter-day. And immediately it *was* quarter-day; and the King's quarter's salary came rattling down the chimney, and bounced into the middle of the floor.

But this was not half of what happened – no, not a quarter; for immediately afterwards the good Fairy Grandmarina came riding in, in a carriage and four (peacocks), with Mr Pickles's boy up behind, dressed in silver and gold, with a cocked hat, powdered hair, pink silk stockings, a jewelled cane and a nosegay. Down jumped Mr Pickles's boy, with his cocked hat in his hand, and wonderfully polite (being entirely changed by enchantment), and handed Grandmarina out; and there she stood, in her rich shot silk smelling of dried lavender, fanning herself with a sparkling fan.

"Alicia, my dear," said this charming old fairy, "how do you do? I hope I see you pretty well? Give me a kiss."

The Princess Alicia embraced her; and then Grandmarina turned to the King, and said rather sharply, "Are you good?"

The King said he hoped so.

"I suppose you know the reason *now*, why my goddaughter here," kissing the princess again, "did not apply to the fishbone sooner?" said the fairy.

The King made a shy bow.

"Ah! But you didn't *then*?" said the fairy.

The King made a shyer bow.

"Any more reasons to ask for?" said the fairy.

The King said no, and he was very sorry.

"Be good, then," said the fairy, "and live happy ever afterwards."

Then Grandmarina waved her fan, and the Queen came in most splendidly dressed; and the seventeen young princes and princesses, no longer grown out of their clothes, came in, newly fitted out from top to toe, with tucks in everything to admit of its being let out. After that, the fairy tapped the Princess Alicia with her fan; and the smothering coarse apron flew away, and she appeared exquisitely dressed, like a little bride, with a wreath of orange flowers and a silver veil. After that, the kitchen dresser changed of itself into a wardrobe, made of beautiful woods and gold and looking glass, which was full of dresses of all sorts, all for her and all exactly fitting her. After that, the angelic baby came in, running alone, with his face and eye not a bit the worse, but much the better. Then Grandmarina begged to be introduced to the duchess; and, when the duchess was brought down, many compliments passed between them.

A little whispering took place between the fairy and the duchess; and then the fairy said out loud, "Yes, I thought she would have told you." Grandmarina then turned to the King and Queen, and said, "We are going in search of Prince Certainpersonio. The pleasure of your company is requested at church in half an hour precisely. So she and the Princess Alicia got into the carriage; and Mr Pickles's boy handed in the duchess, who sat by herself on the opposite seat; and then Mr Pickles's boy put up the steps and got up behind, and the peacocks flew away with their tails behind.

Prince Certainpersonio was sitting by himself, eating barley sugar, and waiting to be ninety. When he saw the peacocks, followed by the carriage, coming in at the window, it immediately occurred to him that something uncommon was going to happen.

"Prince," said Grandmarina, "I bring you your bride."

The moment the fairy said those words, Prince Certainpersonio's face left off being sticky, and his jacket and corduroys changed to peach-bloom velvet, and his hair curled, and a cap and feather flew in like a bird and settled on his head. He got into the carriage by the fairy's invitation; and there he renewed his acquaintance with the duchess, whom he had seen before.

In the church were the prince's relations and friends, and the Princess Alicia's relations and friends, and the seventeen princes and princesses, and the baby, and a crowd of the neighbours.

The marriage was beautiful beyond expression. The duchess was bridesmaid, and beheld the ceremony from the pulpit, where she was supported by the cushion of the desk.

Grandmarina gave a magnificent wedding feast afterwards, in which there was everything and more to eat, and everything and more to drink. The wedding cake was delicately ornamented with white satin ribbons, frosted silver and white lilies, and was forty-two yards round.

When Grandmarina had drunk her love to the young couple, and Prince Certainpersonio had made a speech, and everybody had cried, "Hip, hip, hip, hurrah!" – Grandmarina announced to the King and Queen that in future there would be eight quarter-days in every year, except in leap year, when there would be ten. She then turned to Certainpersonio and Alicia, and said, "My dears, you will have thirty-five children, and they will all be good and beautiful. Seventeen of your children will be boys, and eighteen will be girls. The hair of the whole of your children will curl naturally. They will never have the measles, and will have recovered from the whooping cough before being born."

On hearing such good news, everybody cried out "Hip, hip, hip, hurrah!" again.

"It only remains," said Grandmarina in conclusion, "to make an end of the fishbone."

So she took it from the hand of the Princess Alicia, and it instantly flew down the throat of the dreadful little snapping pug dog next door, and choked him, and he expired in convulsions.

Part III

ROMANCE. FROM THE PEN OF LIEUT. COL. ROBIN REDFORTH*

THE SUBJECT OF OUR PRESENT NARRATIVE would appear to have devoted himself to the pirate profession at a comparatively early age. We find him in command of a splendid schooner of one hundred guns loaded to the muzzle, ere yet he had had a party in honour of his tenth birthday.

It seems that our hero, considering himself spited by a Latin-grammar master, demanded the satisfaction due from one man of honour to another. Not getting it, he privately withdrew his haughty spirit from such low company, bought a second-hand pocket pistol, folded up some sandwiches in a paper bag, made a bottle of Spanish liquorice water and entered on a career of valour.

It were tedious to follow Boldheart (for such was his name) through the commencing stages of his story. Suffice it that we find him bearing the rank of Capt. Boldheart, reclining in full uniform on a crimson hearthrug spread out upon the quarter-deck of his schooner *The Beauty*, in the China seas. It was a lovely evening; and, as his crew lay grouped about him, he favoured them with the following melody:

O landsmen are folly!
O pirates are jolly!
O diddleum Dolly,

Di.

Chorus. – Heave yo.

The soothing effect of these animated sounds floating over the waters, as the common sailors united their rough voices to take up the rich tones of Boldheart, may be more easily conceived than described.

It was under these circumstances that the lookout at the masthead gave the word, "Whales!"

All was now activity.

"Where away?" cried Capt. Boldheart, starting up.

"On the larboard bow, sir," replied the fellow at the masthead, touching his hat. For such was the height of discipline on board of *The Beauty* that, even at that height, he was obliged to mind it, or be shot through the head.

"This adventure belongs to me," said Boldheart. "Boy, my harpoon. Let no man follow" – and leaping alone into his boat, the captain rowed with admirable dexterity in the direction of the monster.

All was now excitement.

"He nears him!" said an elderly seaman, following the captain through his spyglass.

"He strikes him!" said another seaman, a mere stripling, but also with a spyglass.

"He tows him towards us!" said another seaman, a man in the full vigour of life, but also with a spyglass.

In fact, the captain was seen approaching, with the huge bulk following. We will not dwell on the deafening cries of "Boldheart! Boldheart!" with which he was received, when, carelessly leaping on the quarter-deck, he presented his prize to his men. They afterwards made two thousand, four hundred and seventeen pound, ten and sixpence by it.

Ordering the sail to be braced up, the captain now stood WNW. *The Beauty* flew rather than floated over the dark blue waters. Nothing particular occurred for a fortnight, except taking, with considerable slaughter, four Spanish galleons, and a snow from South America, all richly laden. Inaction began to tell upon the spirits of the men. Capt. Boldheart called all hands aft, and said, "My lads, I hear there are discontented ones among ye. Let any such stand forth."

After some murmuring, in which the expressions "Ay, ay, Sir!", "Union Jack", "Avast", "Starboard", "Port", "Bowsprit" and similar indications of a mutinous undercurrent, though subdued, were audible, Bill Boozey, captain of the foretop, came out from the rest. His form was that of a giant, but he quailed under the captain's eye.

"What are your wrongs?" said the captain.

"Why, d'ye see, Capt. Boldheart," replied the towering mariner, "I've sailed, man and boy, for many a year, but I never yet know'd the milk served out for the ship's company's teas to be so sour as 'tis aboard this craft."

At this moment the thrilling cry "Man overboard!" announced to the astonished crew that Boozey, in stepping back, as the captain (in mere thoughtfulness) laid his hand upon the faithful pocket pistol which he wore in his belt, had lost his balance, and was struggling with the foaming tide.

All was now stupefaction.

But with Captain Boldheart, to throw off his uniform coat, regardless of the various rich orders with which it was decorated, and to plunge into the sea after the drowning giant, was the work of a moment. Maddening was the excitement when boats were lowered; intense the joy when the captain was seen holding up the drowning man with his teeth; deafening the cheering when both were restored to the main deck of *The Beauty*. And, from the instant of his changing his wet clothes for dry ones, Capt. Boldheart had no such devoted though humble friend as William Boozey.

Boldheart now pointed to the horizon, and called the attention of his crew to the taper spars of a ship lying snug in harbour under the guns of a fort.

"She shall be ours at sunrise," said he. "Serve out a double allowance of grog, and prepare for action."

All was now preparation.

When morning dawned, after a sleepless night, it was seen that the stranger was crowding on all sail to come out of the harbour and offer battle. As the two ships came nearer to each other, the stranger fired a gun and hoisted Roman colours. Boldheart then perceived her to be the Latin-grammar master's bark. Such indeed she was, and had been tacking about the world in unavailing pursuit, from the time of his first taking to a roving life.

Boldheart now addressed his men, promising to blow them up if he should feel convinced that their reputation required it, and giving orders that the Latin-grammar master should be taken alive. He then dismissed them to their quarters, and the fight began with a broadside from *The Beauty*. She then veered around, and poured in another. *The Scorpion* (so was the bark of the Latin-grammar master appropriately called) was not slow to return her fire; and a terrific cannonading ensued, in which the guns of *The Beauty* did tremendous execution.

The Latin-grammar master was seen upon the poop, in the midst of the smoke and fire, encouraging his men. To do him justice, he was no craven, though his white hat, his short grey trousers and his long snuff-coloured surtout reaching to his heels (the selfsame coat in which he had spited Boldheart), contrasted most unfavourably with the brilliant uniform of the latter. At this moment, Boldheart, seizing a pike and putting himself at the head of his men, gave the word to board.

A desperate conflict ensued in the hammock nettings – or somewhere in about that direction – until the Latin-grammar master, having all his masts gone, his hull and rigging shot through, and seeing Boldheart slashing a path towards him, hauled down his flag himself, gave up his sword to Boldheart, and asked for quarter. Scarce had he been put into the captain's boat, ere *The Scorpion* went down with all on board.

On Capt. Boldheart's now assembling his men, a circumstance occurred. He found it necessary with one blow of his cutlass to kill the cook, who, having lost his brother in the late action, was making at the Latin-grammar master in an infuriated state, intent on his destruction with a carving knife.

Capt. Boldheart then turned to the Latin-grammar master, severely reproaching him with his perfidy, and put it to his crew what they considered that a master who spited a boy deserved.

They answered with one voice, "Death."

"It may be so," said the captain, "but it shall never be said that Boldheart stained his hour of triumph with the blood of his enemy. Prepare the cutter."

The cutter was immediately prepared.

"Without taking your life," said the captain, "I must yet for ever deprive you of the power of spiting other boys. I shall turn you adrift in this boat. You will find in her two oars, a compass, a bottle of rum, a small cask of water, a piece of pork, a bag of biscuits and my Latin grammar. Go! – and spite the natives, if you can find any."

Deeply conscious of this bitter sarcasm, the unhappy wretch was put into the cutter, and was soon left far behind. He made no effort to row, but was seen lying on his back with his legs up, when last made out by the ship's telescopes.

A stiff breeze now beginning to blow, Capt. Boldheart gave orders to keep her SSW, easing her a little during the night by falling off a point or two W by W, or even by WS, if she complained much. He then retired for the night, having in truth much need of repose. In addition to the fatigues he had undergone, this brave officer had received sixteen wounds in the engagement, but had not mentioned it.

In the morning a white squall came on, and was succeeded by other squalls of various colours. It thundered and lightened heavily for six weeks. Hurricanes then set in for two months. Waterspouts and tornadoes followed. The oldest sailor on board – and he was a very old one – had never seen such weather. *The Beauty* lost all idea where she was, and the carpenter reported six feet two of water in the hold. Everybody fell senseless at the pumps every day.

Provisions now ran very low. Our hero put the crew on short allowance, and put himself on shorter allowance than any man in the ship. But his spirit kept him fat. In this extremity, the gratitude of Boozey, the captain of the foretop, whom our readers may remember, was truly affecting. The loving though lowly William repeatedly requested to be killed, and preserved for the captain's table.

We now approach a change of affairs.

One day during a gleam of sunshine, and when the weather had moderated, the man at the masthead – too weak now to touch his hat, besides its having been blown away – called out, "Savages!"

All was now expectation.

Presently fifteen hundred canoes, each paddled by twenty savages, were seen advancing in excellent order. They were of a light-green colour (the savages were), and sang, with great energy, the following strain:

Choo a choo a choo tooth.

Muntch, muntch. Nycey!

Choo a choo a choo tooth.

Muntch, muntch. Nycey!

As the shades of night were by this time closing in, these expressions were supposed to embody this simple people's views of the evening hymn. But it too soon appeared that the song was a translation of "For what we are going to receive" etc.

The chief, imposingly decorated with feathers of lively colours, and having the majestic appearance of a fighting parrot, no sooner understood (he understood English perfectly) that the ship was *The Beauty*, Capt. Boldheart, than he fell upon his face on the deck, and could not be persuaded to rise until the captain had lifted him up, and told him he wouldn't hurt him. All the rest of the savages also fell on their faces with marks of terror, and had also to be lifted up one by one. Thus the fame of the great Boldheart had gone before him, even among these children of Nature.

Turtles and oysters were now produced in astonishing numbers, and on these and yams the people made a hearty meal. After dinner the chief told Capt. Boldheart that there was better feeding up at the village, and that he would be glad to take him and his officers there. Apprehensive of treachery, Boldheart ordered his boat's crew to attend him completely armed. And well were it for other commanders if their precautions – but let us not anticipate.

When the canoes arrived at the beach, the darkness of the night was illumined by the light of an immense fire. Ordering his boat's crew (with the intrepid though illiterate William at their head) to keep close and be upon their guard, Boldheart bravely went on, arm in arm with the chief.

But how to depict the captain's surprise when he found a ring of savages singing in chorus that barbarous translation of "For what we are going to receive" etc., which has been given above, and dancing hand in hand round the Latin-grammar master, in a hamper with his head shaved, while two savages floured him, before putting him to the fire to be cooked!

Boldheart now took counsel with his officers on the course to be adopted. In the meantime, the miserable captive never ceased begging pardon and imploring to be delivered. On the generous Boldheart's proposal, it was at length resolved that he should not be cooked, but should be allowed to remain raw, on two conditions, namely:

1. That he should never, under any circumstances, presume to teach any boy anything any more.

2. That, if taken back to England, he should pass his life in travelling to find out boys who wanted their exercises done, and should do their exercises for those boys for nothing, and never say a word about it.

Drawing the sword from its sheath, Boldheart swore him to these conditions on its shining blade. The prisoner wept bitterly, and appeared acutely to feel the errors of his past career.

The captain then ordered his boat's crew to make ready for a volley, and after firing to reload quickly. "And expect a score or two on ye to go head over heels," murmured William Boozey, "for I'm a-looking at ye." With those words, the derisive though deadly William took a good aim.

"Fire!"

The ringing voice of Boldheart was lost in the report of the guns and the screeching of the savages. Volley after volley awakened the numerous echoes. Hundreds of savages were killed, hundreds wounded, and thousands ran howling into the woods. The Latin-grammar master had a spare nightcap lent him, and a longtail coat, which he wore hind side before. He presented a ludicrous though pitiable appearance, and serve him right.

We now find Capt. Boldheart, with this rescued wretch on board, standing off for other islands. At one of these, not a cannibal island, but a pork and vegetable one, he married (only in fun on his part) the King's daughter. Here he rested some time, receiving from the natives great quantities of precious stones, gold dust, elephants' teeth and sandalwood, and getting very rich. This, too, though he almost every day made presents of enormous value to his men.

The ship being at length as full as she could hold of all sorts of valuable things, Boldheart gave orders to weigh the anchor, and turn *The Beauty*'s head towards England. These orders were obeyed with three cheers; and ere the sun went down full many a hornpipe had been danced on deck by the uncouth though agile William.

We next find Capt. Boldheart about three leagues off Madeira, surveying through his spyglass a stranger of suspicious appearance making sail towards him. On his firing a gun ahead of her to bring her to, she ran up a flag, which he instantly recognized as the flag from the mast in the back garden at home.

Inferring from this that his father had put to sea to seek his long-lost son, the captain sent his own boat on board the stranger to enquire if this was so and, if so, whether his father's intentions were strictly honourable. The boat came back with a present of greens and fresh meat, and reported that the stranger was *The Family*, of twelve hundred tons, and had not only the captain's father on board, but also his mother, with the majority of his aunts and uncles, and all his cousins. It was further reported to Boldheart that the whole of these relations had expressed themselves in a becoming manner, and were anxious to embrace him and thank him for the glorious credit he had done them. Boldheart at once invited them to breakfast next morning on board *The Beauty*, and gave orders for a brilliant ball that should last all day.

It was in the course of the night that the captain discovered the hopelessness of reclaiming the Latin-grammar master. That thankless traitor was found out, as the two ships lay near each other, communicating with *The Family* by signals, and offering to give up Boldheart. He was hanged at the yardarm the first thing in the morning, after having it impressively pointed out to him by Boldheart that this was what spiters came to.

The meeting between the captain and his parents was attended with tears. His uncles and aunts would have attended their meeting with tears too, but he wasn't going to stand that. His cousins were very much astonished by the size of his ship and the discipline of his men, and were greatly overcome by the splendour of his uniform. He kindly conducted them round the vessel, and pointed out everything worthy of notice. He also fired his hundred guns, and found it amusing to witness their alarm.

The entertainment surpassed everything ever seen on board ship, and lasted from ten in the morning until seven the next morning. Only one disagreeable incident occurred. Capt. Boldheart found himself obliged to put his cousin Tom in irons, for being disrespectful. On the boy's promising amendment, however, he was humanely released after a few hours' close confinement.

Boldheart now took his mother down into the great cabin, and asked after the young lady with whom, it was well known to the world, he was in love. His mother replied that the object of his affections was then at school at Margate, for the benefit of sea-bathing (it was the month of September), but that she feared the young lady's friends were still opposed to the union. Boldheart at once resolved, if necessary, to bombard the town.

Taking the command of his ship with this intention, and putting all but fighting men on board *The Family*, with orders to that vessel to keep in company, Boldheart soon anchored in Margate Roads. Here he went ashore well-armed, and attended by his boat's crew (at their head the faithful though ferocious

William), and demanded to see the mayor, who came out of his office.

"Dost know the name of yon ship, mayor?" asked Boldheart fiercely.

"No," said the mayor, rubbing his eyes, which he could scarce believe, when he saw the goodly vessel riding at anchor.

"She is named *The Beauty*," said the captain.

"Hah!" exclaimed the mayor, with a start. "And you, then, are Capt. Boldheart?"

"The same."

A pause ensued. The mayor trembled.

"Now, mayor," said the captain, "choose! Help me to my bride, or be bombarded."

The mayor begged for two hours' grace, in which to make enquiries respecting the young lady. Boldheart accorded him but one, and during that one placed William Boozey sentry over him, with a drawn sword, and instructions to accompany him wherever he went, and to run him through the body if he showed a sign of playing false.

At the end of the hour the mayor reappeared more dead than alive, closely waited on by Boozey more alive than dead.

"Captain," said the mayor, "I have ascertained that the young lady is going to bathe. Even now she waits her turn for a machine. The tide is low, though rising. I, in one of our town boats, shall not be suspected. When she comes forth in her bathing dress into the shallow water from behind the hood of the machine, my boat shall intercept her and prevent her return. Do you the rest."

"Mayor," returned Capt. Boldheart, "thou hast saved thy town."

The captain then signalled his boat to take him off and, steering her himself, ordered her crew to row towards the bathing ground, and there to rest upon their oars. All happened as had been arranged. His lovely bride came forth, the mayor glided in behind her, she became confused and had floated out of her depth when, with one skilful touch of the rudder and one quivering stroke from the boat's crew, her adoring Boldheart held her in his strong arms. There her shrieks of terror were changed to cries of joy.

Before *The Beauty* could get under way, the hoisting of all the flags in the town and harbour, and the ringing of all the bells, announced to the brave Boldheart that he had nothing to fear. He therefore determined to be married on the spot, and signalled for a clergyman and clerk, who came off promptly in a sailing boat named *The Skylark*. Another great entertainment was then given on board *The Beauty*, in the midst of which the mayor was called out by a messenger. He returned with the news that government had sent down to know whether Capt. Boldheart, in acknowledgement of the great services he had done his country by being a pirate, would consent to be made a lieutenant colonel. For himself he would have spurned the worthless boon; but his bride wished it, and he consented.

Only one thing further happened before the good ship *Family* was dismissed, with rich presents to all on board. It is painful to record (but such is human nature in some cousins) that

Capt. Boldheart's unmannerly Cousin Tom was actually tied up to receive three dozen with a rope's end "for cheekiness and making game", when Capt. Boldheart's lady begged for him, and he was spared. *The Beauty* then refitted, and the captain and his bride departed for the Indian Ocean to enjoy themselves for evermore.

Part IV

ROMANCE. FROM THE PEN OF MISS NETTIE ASHFORD*

T HERE IS A COUNTRY, which I will show you when I get into maps, where the children have everything their own way. It is a most delightful country to live in. The grown-up people are obliged to obey the children, and are never allowed to sit up to supper, except on their birthdays. The children order them to make jam and jelly and marmalade, and tarts and pies and puddings, and all manner of pastry. If they say they won't, they are put in the corner till they do. They are sometimes allowed to have some; but when they have some, they generally have powders given them afterwards.

One of the inhabitants of this country, a truly sweet young crea-ture of the name of Mrs Orange, had the misfortune to be sadly plagued by her numerous family. Her parents required a great deal of looking after, and they had connections and companions who were scarcely ever out of mischief. So Mrs Orange said to herself, "I really cannot be troubled with these torments any longer: I must put them all to school."

Mrs Orange took off her pinafore, and dressed herself very nicely and took up her baby, and went out to call upon another lady of the name of Mrs Lemon, who kept a preparatory establishment. Mrs Orange stood upon the scraper to pull at the bell, and give a ring-ting-ting.

Mrs Lemon's neat little housemaid, pulling up her socks as she came along the passage, answered the ring-ting-ting.

"Good morning," said Mrs Orange. "Fine day. How do you do? Mrs Lemon at home?"

"Yes, ma'am."

"Will you say Mrs Orange and baby?"

"Yes, ma'am. Walk in."

Mrs Orange's baby was a very fine one, and real wax all over. Mrs Lemon's baby was leather and bran. However, when Mrs Lemon came into the drawing room with her baby in her arms, Mrs Orange said politely, "Good morning. Fine day. How do you do? And how is little Tootleum-boots?"

"Well, she is but poorly. Cutting her teeth, ma'am," said Mrs Lemon.

"Oh, indeed, ma'am!" said Mrs Orange. "No fits, I hope?"

"No, ma'am."

"How many teeth has she, ma'am?"

"Five, ma'am."

"My Emilia, ma'am, has eight," said Mrs Orange. "Shall we lay them on the mantelpiece side by side, while we converse?"

"By all means, ma'am," said Mrs Lemon. "Hem!"

"The first question is, ma'am," said Mrs Orange, "I don't bore you?"

"Not in the least, ma'am," said Mrs Lemon. "Far from it, I assure you."

"Then pray *have* you," said Mrs Orange, "*have* you any vacancies?"

"Yes, ma'am. How many might you require?"

"Why, the truth is, ma'am," said Mrs Orange, "I have come to the conclusion that my children" – oh, I forgot to say that they call the grown-up people children in that country! – "that my children are getting positively too much for me. Let me see. Two parents, two intimate friends of theirs, one godfather, two godmothers and an aunt. *Have* you as many as eight vacancies?"

"I have just eight, ma'am," said Mrs Lemon.

"Most fortunate! Terms moderate, I think?"

"Very moderate, ma'am."

"Diet good, I believe?"

"Excellent, ma'am."

"Unlimited?"

"Unlimited."

"Most satisfactory! Corporal punishment dispensed with?"

"Why, we do occasionally shake," said Mrs Lemon, "and we have slapped. But only in extreme cases."

"*Could* I, ma'am," said Mrs Orange, "*could* I see the establishment?"

"With the greatest of pleasure, ma'am," said Mrs Lemon. Mrs Lemon took Mrs Orange into the schoolroom, where there were a number of pupils. "Stand up, children," said Mrs Lemon; and they all stood up.

Mrs Orange whispered to Mrs Lemon, "There is a pale, bald child, with red whiskers, in disgrace. Might I ask what he has done?"

"Come here, White," said Mrs Lemon, "and tell this lady what you have been doing."

"Betting on horses," said White sulkily.

"Are you sorry for it, you naughty child?" said Mrs Lemon.

"No," said White. "Sorry to lose, but shouldn't be sorry to win."

"There's a vicious boy for you, ma'am," said Mrs Lemon. "Go along with you, sir. This is Brown, Mrs Orange. Oh, a sad case, Brown's! Never knows when he has had enough. Greedy. How is your gout, sir?"

"Bad," said Brown.

"What else can you expect?" said Mrs Lemon. "Your stomach is the size of two. Go and take exercise directly. Mrs Black, come here to me. Now, here is a child, Mrs Orange, ma'am, who is always at play. She can't be kept at home a single day together; always gadding about and spoiling her clothes. Play, play, play, play, from morning to night, and to morning again. How can she expect to improve?"

"Don't expect to improve," sulked Mrs Black. "Don't want to."

"There is a specimen of her temper, ma'am," said Mrs Lemon. "To see her when she is tearing about, neglecting everything else, you would suppose her to be at least good-humoured. But bless you! – ma'am, she is as pert and flouncing a minx as ever you met with in all your days!"

"You must have a great deal of trouble with them, ma'am," said Mrs Orange.

"Ah, I have, indeed, ma'am!" said Mrs Lemon. "What with their tempers, what with their quarrels, what with their never knowing what's good for them, and what with their always wanting to domineer, deliver me from these unreasonable children!"

"Well, I wish you good morning, ma'am," said Mrs Orange.

"Well, I wish you good morning, ma'am," said Mrs Lemon.

So Mrs Orange took up her baby and went home, and told the family that plagued her so that they were all going to be sent to school. They said they didn't want to go to school; but she packed up their boxes, and packed them off.

"Oh dear me, dear me! Rest and be thankful!" said Mrs Orange, throwing herself back in her little armchair. "Those troublesome troubles are got rid of, please the pigs!"

Just then another lady, named Mrs Alicumpaine, came calling at the street door with a ring-ting-ting.

"My dear Mrs Alicumpaine," said Mrs Orange, "how do you do? Pray stay to dinner. We have but a simple joint of sweet stuff, followed by a plain dish of bread and treacle; but, if you will take us as you find us, it will be *so* kind!"

"Don't mention it," said Mrs Alicumpaine. "I shall be too glad. But what do you think I have come for, ma'am? Guess, ma'am."

"I really cannot guess, ma'am," said Mrs Orange.

"Why, I am going to have a small juvenile party tonight," said Mrs Alicumpaine, "and if you and Mr Orange and baby would but join us, we should be complete."

"More than charmed, I am sure!" said Mrs Orange.

"So kind of you!" said Mrs Alicumpaine. "But I hope the children won't bore you!"

"Dear things! Not at all," said Mrs Orange. "I dote upon them."

Mr Orange here came home from the city; and he came, too, with a ring-ting-ting.

"James, love," said Mrs Orange, "you look tired. What has been doing in the city today?"

"Trap, bat and ball, my dear," said Mr Orange, "and it knocks a man up."

"That dreadfully anxious city, ma'am," said Mrs Orange to Mrs Alicumpaine, "so wearing, is it not?"

"Oh, so trying!" said Mrs Alicumpaine. "John has lately been speculating in the peg-top ring; and I often say to him at night, 'John, *is* the result worth the wear and tear?'"

Dinner was ready by this time: so they sat down to dinner; and while Mr Orange carved the joint of sweet stuff, he said, "It's a poor heart that never rejoices. Jane, go down to the cellar, and fetch a bottle of the Upest ginger beer."

At teatime, Mr and Mrs Orange, and baby, and Mrs Alicumpaine went off to Mrs Alicumpaine's house. The children had not come yet; but the ballroom was ready for them, decorated with paper flowers.

"How very sweet!" said Mrs Orange. "The dear things! How pleased they will be!"

"I don't care for children myself," said Mr Orange, gaping.

"Not for girls?" said Mrs Alicumpaine. "Come! You care for girls?"

Mr Orange shook his head, and gaped again. "Frivolous and vain, ma'am."

"My dear James," cried Mrs Orange, who had been peeping about, "do look here. Here's the supper for the darlings, ready laid in the room behind the folding doors. Here's their little pickled salmon, I do declare! And here's their little salad, and their little roast beef and fowls, and their little pastry, and their wee, wee, wee champagne!"

"Yes, I thought it best, ma'am," said Mrs Alicumpaine, "that they should have their supper by themselves. Our table is in the corner here, where the gentlemen can have their wineglass of negus, and their egg sandwich, and their quiet game at beggar-my-neighbour, and look on. As for us, ma'am, we shall have quite enough to do to manage the company."

"Oh, indeed, you may say so! Quite enough, ma'am," said Mrs Orange.

The company began to come. The first of them was a stout boy, with a white topknot and spectacles. The housemaid brought him in and said, "Compliments, and at what time was he to be fetched?" Mrs Alicumpaine said, "Not a moment later than ten. How do you do, sir? Go and sit down." Then a number of other children came; boys by themselves, and girls by themselves, and boys and girls together. They didn't behave at all well. Some of them looked through quizzing glasses at others, and said, "Who are those? Don't know them." Some of them looked through quizzing glasses at others, and said, "How do?" Some of them had cups of tea or coffee handed to them by others, and said, "Thanks, much!" A good many boys stood about, and felt their shirt collars. Four tiresome fat boys *would* stand in the doorway, and talk about the newspapers, till Mrs Alicumpaine went to them and said, "My dears, I really cannot allow you to prevent people from coming in. I shall be truly sorry to do it; but, if you put yourself in everybody's way, I must positively send you home." One boy, with a heard and a large white waistcoat, who stood straddling on the hearthrug warming his coat tails, *was* sent home. "Highly incorrect, my dear," said Mrs Alicumpaine, handing him out of the room, "and I cannot permit it."

There was a children's hand – harp, cornet and piano – and Mrs Alicumpaine and Mrs Orange hustled among the children to persuade them to take partners and dance. But they were so obstinate! For quite a long time they would not he persuaded to take partners and dance. Most of the boys said, "Thanks, much! But not at present." And most of the rest of the boys said, "Thanks, much! But never do."

"Oh, these children are very wearing!" said Mrs Alicumpaine to Mrs Orange.

"Dear things! I dote upon them; but they ARE wearing," said Mrs Orange to Mrs Alicumpaine.

At last they did begin in a slow and melancholy way to slide about to the music: though even then they wouldn't mind what they were told, but would have this partner, and wouldn't have that partner, and showed temper about it. And they wouldn't smile – no, not on any account they wouldn't; but, when the music stopped, went round and round the room in dismal twos, as if everybody else was dead.

"Oh, it's very hard indeed to get these vexing children to be entertained!" said Mrs Alicumpaine to Mrs Orange.

"I dote upon the darlings; but it IS hard," said Mrs Orange to Mrs Alicumpaine.

They were trying children, that's the truth. First, they wouldn't sing when they were asked; and then, when everybody fully believed they wouldn't, they would. "If you serve us so any more, my love," said Mrs Alicumpaine to a tall child, with a good deal of white back, in mauve silk trimmed with lace, "it will be my painful privilege to offer you a bed, and to send you to it immediately."

The girls were so ridiculously dressed, too, that they were in rags before supper. How could the boys help treading on their trains? And yet when their trains were trodden on, they often showed temper again, and looked as black, they did! However, they all seemed to be pleased when Mrs Alicumpaine said, "Supper is ready, children!" And they went crowding and pushing in, as if they had had dry bread for dinner.

"How are the children getting on?" said Mr Orange to Mrs Orange, when Mrs Orange came to look after baby. Mrs Orange had left baby on a shelf near Mr Orange while he played at beggar-my-neighbour, and had asked him to keep his eye upon her now and then.

"Most charmingly, my dear!" said Mrs Orange. "So droll to see their little flirtations and jealousies! Do come and look!"

"Much obliged to you, my dear," said Mr Orange, "but I don't care about children myself."

So Mrs Orange, having seen that baby was safe, went back without Mr Orange to the room where the children were having supper.

"What are they doing now?" said Mrs Orange to Mrs Alicumpaine.

"They are making speeches, and playing at parliament," said Mrs Alicumpaine to Mrs Orange.

On hearing this, Mrs Orange set off once more back again to Mr Orange, and said, "James dear, do come. The children are playing at parliament."

"Thank you, my dear," said Mr Orange, "but I don't care about parliament myself."

So Mrs Orange went once again without Mr Orange to the room where the children were having supper, to see them playing at parliament. And she found some of the boys crying, "Hear, hear, hear!" while other boys cried "No, no!" and others "Question!", "Spoke!" and all sorts of nonsense that ever you heard. Then one of those tiresome fat boys who had stopped the doorway told them he was on his legs (as if they couldn't see that he wasn't on his head, or on his anything else) to explain, and that, with the permission of his honourable friend, if he would allow him to call him so (another tiresome boy bowed), he would proceed to explain. Then he went on for a long time in a sing-song (whatever he meant), did this troublesome fat boy, about that he held in his hand a glass; and about that he had come down to that house that night to discharge what he would call a public duty; and about that, on the present occasion, he would lay his hand (his other hand) upon his heart, and would tell honourable gentlemen that he was about to open the door to general approval. Then he opened the door by saying, "To our hostess!" and everybody else said "To our hostess!" and then there were cheers. Then another tiresome boy started up in sing-song, and then half a dozen noisy and nonsensical boys at once. But at last Mrs Alicumpaine said, "I cannot have this din. Now, children, you have played at parliament very nicely; but parliament gets tiresome after a little while, and it's time you left off, for you will soon be fetched."

After another dance (with more tearing to rags than before supper), they began to be fetched; and you will be very glad to be told that the tiresome fat boy who had been on his legs was walked off first without any ceremony. When they were all gone, poor Mrs Alicumpaine dropped upon a sofa, and said to Mrs Orange, "These children will be the death of me at last, ma'am, – they will indeed!"

"I quite adore them, ma'am," said Mrs Orange, "but they DO want variety."

Mr Orange got his hat, and Mrs Orange got her bonnet and her baby, and they set out to walk home. They had to pass Mrs Lemon's preparatory establishment on their way.

"I wonder, James dear," said Mrs Orange, looking up at the window, "whether the precious children are asleep!"

"I don't care much whether they are or not, myself," said Mr Orange.

"James dear!"

"You dote upon them, you know," said Mr Orange. "That's another thing."

"I do," said Mrs Orange rapturously. "Oh, I DO!"

"I don't," said Mr Orange.

"But I was thinking, James love," said Mrs Orange, pressing his arm, "whether our dear, good, kind Mrs Lemon would like them to stay the holidays with her."

"If she was paid for it, I daresay she would," said Mr Orange.

"I adore them, James," said Mrs Orange, "but SUPPOSE we pay her, then!"

This was what brought that country to such perfection, and made it such a delightful place to live in. The grown-up people (that would be in other countries) soon left off being allowed any holidays after Mr and Mrs Orange tried the experiment; and the children (that would be in other countries) kept them at school as long as ever they lived, and made them do whatever they were told.

Note on the Texts

The texts in the present edition are based on those contained in the Fireside Dickens edition of *Hard Times, Hunted Down, Holiday Romance & George Silverman's Explanation* (London: Chapman & Hall Ltd and Henry Frowde, *c.*1914). The spelling and punctuation have been standardized, modernized and made consistent throughout.

Notes

p. 15, *scrambling board*: A "scrambling" meal is one at which one helps oneself to whatever one can get.

p. 25, *DV*: *Deo volente*: "God willing" (Latin).

p. 34, *Lady Jane Grey*: Lady Jane Grey (1536/37–54), a noblewoman and briefly the de-facto Queen of England, was considered a model of humanist learning.

p. 81, *Introductory Romance… William Tinkling, Esq.*: Aged eight. (AUTHOR'S NOTE)

p. 93, *Romance. From the Pen of Miss Alice Rainbird*: Aged seven. (AUTHOR'S NOTE)

p. 93, *quarter-day*: One of four dates in the year on which, among other things, rents were traditionally due.

p. 107, *Romance. From the Pen of Lieut. Col. Robin Redforth*: Aged nine. (AUTHOR'S NOTE)

p. 121, *Romance. From the Pen of Miss Nettie Ashford*: Aged half-past six. (AUTHOR'S NOTE)

Extra Material

on

Charles Dickens's

George Silverman's Explanation

Charles Dickens's Life

Charles John Huffam Dickens was born in Portsmouth on 7th *First Years*
February 1812 to John Dickens and Elizabeth Dickens, née Barrow.
His father worked as a navy payroll clerk at the local dockyard,
before transferring and moving his family to London in 1814,
and then to Kent in 1817. It seems that this period possessed
an idyllic atmosphere for ever afterwards in Dickens's mind.
Much of his childhood was spent reading and rereading the
books in his father's library, which included *Robinson Crusoe*,
The Vicar of Wakefield, *Don Quixote*, Fielding, Smollett and
the *Arabian Nights*. He was a promising, prize-winning pupil
at school, and generally distinguished by his cleverness, sensitiv-
ity and enthusiasm, although unfortunately this was tempered
by his frail and sickly constitution. It was at this time that he
also had his first experience of what would become one of the
abiding passions in his life: the theatre. Sadly, John Dickens's
finances had become increasingly unhealthy, a situation which
was worsened when he was transferred to London in 1822. This
relocation, which entailed a termination in his schooling, dis-
tressed Charles, though he slowly came to be fascinated with
the teeming, squalid streets of London.

In London, however, family finances continued to plummet *Bankruptcy*
until the Dickenses were facing bankruptcy. A family connection, *and the*
James Lamert, offered to employ Charles at the Warren's Blacking *Warehouse*
Warehouse, which he was managing, and Dickens started working
there in February 1824. He spent between six months and a year
there, and the experience would prove to have a profound and
lasting effect on him. The work was drudgery – sealing and label-
ling pots of black paste all day – and his only companions were
uneducated working-class boys. His discontent at the situation was
compounded by the fact that his talented older sister was sent to
the Royal Academy of Music, while he was left in the warehouse.

John Dickens was finally arrested for debt and taken to Mar-
shalsea Prison in Southwark on 20th February 1824, his wife and 137

children (excluding Charles) moving in with him in order to save money. Meanwhile, Charles found lodgings with an intimidating old lady called Mrs Roylance (on whom he apparently modelled Mrs Pipchin in *Dombey and Son*) in Little College Street, later moving to Lant Street in Borough, which was closer to the prison. At the end of May 1824, John Dickens was released, and gradually paid off creditors as he attempted to start a new life for himself and his family. However, for some time afterwards Charles reluctantly pursued his employment at the blacking factory, as it seems his mother was unwilling to take him out of it, and even tried to arrange for him to return after he did leave. It appears that he was only removed from the warehouse after his father had quarrelled with James Lamert. The stint at the blacking factory was so profoundly humiliating for Dickens that throughout his life he apparently never mentioned this experience to any of those close to him, revealing it only in a fragment of a memoir written in 1848 and presented to his biographer John Forster: "No words can express the secret agony of my soul as I sunk into this companionship, compared these everyday associates with those of my happier childhood, and felt my early hopes of growing up to be a learned and distinguished man crushed in my breast."

School and Work in London Fortunately he was granted some respite from hard labour when he was sent to be educated at the Wellington House Academy on Hampstead Road. Although the standard of teaching he received was apparently mediocre, the two years he spent at the school were idyllic compared to his warehouse experience, and Charles took advantage of them by making friends his own age and participating in school drama. Regrettably he had to leave the Academy in 1827, when the family finances were in turmoil once again. He found employment as a junior clerk in a solicitor's office, a job that, although routine and somewhat unfulfilling, enabled Dickens to become familiar with the ways of the London courts and the jargon of the legal profession – which he would later frequently lampoon in his novels. On reaching his eighteenth birthday, Dickens enrolled as a reader at the British Museum, determined to make up for the inadequacies of his education by studying the books in its collection, and taught himself shorthand in the hope of taking on journalistic work.

In less than a year he set himself up as a freelance law reporter, initially covering the civil law courts known as Doctors' Commons – which he did with some brio, though he found it slightly tedious – and in 1831 advanced to the press gallery of the House of Commons. His reputation as a reporter was growing steadily, and in 1834 he joined the staff of the *Morning Chronicle*, one of the leading daily newspapers. During this period, he observed and commented on some of the most socially significant debates of the time, such as the Reform Act of 1832, the Factory Act of 1833 and the Poor Law Amendment Act of 1834.

In 1829, he fell in love with the flirtatious and beautiful Maria Beadnell, the daughter of a wealthy banker, and he seems to have remained fixated on her for several years, although she rebuffed his advances. This disappointment spurred him on to achieve a higher station in life, and – after briefly entertaining the notion of becoming an actor – he threw himself into his work and wrote short stories in his spare time, which he had published in magazines, although without pay.

First Love

Soon enough his work for the *Morning Chronicle* was not limited to covering parliamentary matters: in recognition of his capacity for descriptive writing, he was encouraged to write reviews and sketches, and cover important meetings, dinners and election campaigns – which he reported on with enthusiasm. Written under the pseudonym "Boz", his sketches on London street life – published in the *Morning Chronicle* and then also in its sister paper, the *Evening Chronicle* – were highly rated and gained a popular following. Things were also looking up in Dickens's personal life, as he fell in love with Catherine Hogarth, the daughter of the editor of the *Evening Chronicle*: they became engaged in May 1835, and married on 2nd April 1836 at St Luke's Church in Chelsea, honeymooning in Kent afterwards. At this time his literary career began to gain momentum: first his writings on London were compiled under the title *Sketches by Boz* and printed in an illustrated two-volume edition, and then, just a few days before his wedding, *The Pickwick Papers* began to be published in monthly instalments – becoming the best-selling serialization since Lord Byron's *Childe Harold's Pilgrimage*.

Marriage and First Major Publication

At the end of 1836, Dickens resigned from the *Morning Chronicle* to concentrate on his literary endeavours, and met John Forster, who was to remain a lifelong friend. He helped Dickens to manage the business and legal side of his life, as well as acting as a trusted literary adviser and biographer. Forster's acumen for resolving complex situations was particularly welcome at this point, since, following the resounding success of *The Pickwick Papers*, Dickens had over-committed himself to a number of projects, with newspapers and publishers eager to capitalize on the latest literary sensation, and the deals and payments agreed no longer reflected his stature as an author.

Success

In January 1837, Catherine gave birth to the couple's first child, also called Charles, which prompted the young Dickens family to move from their lodgings in Furnival's Inn in Holborn to a house on 48 Doughty Street. The following month *Oliver Twist* started appearing in serial form in *Bentley's Miscellany*, which lifted the author's name to new heights. This period of domestic bliss and professional fulfilment was tragically interrupted when Catherine's sister Mary suddenly died in May at the age of seventeen. Dickens was devastated and had to interrupt work on *The Pickwick Papers* and *Oliver Twist*; this event would have a deep impact on his world view and his art. But his literary productivity would soon continue unabated; hot on the tail of *Oliver Twist* came *Nicholas Nickleby* (1838–39) and *The Old Curiosity Shop* (1840–41). By this stage, he was the leading author of the day, frequenting high society and meeting luminaries such as his idol, Thomas Carlyle. Consequently he moved to a grand Georgian house near Regent's Park, and frequently holidayed in a house in Broadstairs in Kent.

Whereas his previous novels had all more or less followed his successful formula of comedy, melodrama and social satire, Dickens opted for a different approach for his next major work, *Barnaby Rudge*, a purely historical novel. He found the writing of this book particularly arduous, so he decided that after five years of intensive labour he needed a sabbatical, and persuaded his publishers Chapman and Hall to grant him a year's leave with a monthly advance of £150 on his future earnings. During this year he would visit America and keep a notebook on his travels, with a view to getting it published on his return.

First Visit to America   Dickens journeyed by steamship to Halifax, Nova Scotia, accompanied by his wife, in January 1842, and the couple would spend almost five months travelling around North America, visiting cities such as Boston, New York, Philadelphia, Cincinnati, Louisville, Toronto and Montreal. He was greeted by crowds of enthusiastic well-wishers wherever he went, and met countless important figures such as Henry Wadsworth Longfellow, Edgar Allan Poe and President John Tyler, but after the initial exhilaration of this fanfare he found it exhausting and overwhelming. The trip also brought about its share of disillusionment: having cherished romantic dreams of America being free from the corruption and snobbery of Europe, he was increasingly appalled by certain aspects of the New World, such as slavery, the treatment of prisoners and, perhaps most of all, the refusal of America to sign an international copyright agreement to prevent his works being pirated in America. He wrote articles and made speeches condemning these practices, which resulted in a considerable amount of press hostility.

Having returned to England in the summer of 1842, he published *Back Home* his record of the trip under the title of *American Notes* and the first instalment of *Martin Chuzzlewit* later that year. Unfortunately neither of the two were quite as successful as he or his publishers would have hoped, although Dickens believed *Martin Chuzzlewit* (1842–44) was his finest work to date. During this period, Dickens started taking a greater interest in political and social issues, particularly in the treatment of children employed in mines and factories, and in the "ragged school" movement, which provided free education for destitute children. He became acquainted with the millionaire philanthropist Angela Burdett-Coutts, and persuaded her to give financial support to a school in London. In 1843, he decided to write a seasonal tale which would highlight the plight of the poor, publishing *A Christmas Carol* to great popular success in December 1843. The following year Dickens decided to leave Chapman and Hall, as his relations with them had become increasingly strained, and persuaded his printer Bradbury and Evans to become his new publisher.

In July 1844 Dickens relocated his entire family to Genoa in order *Move to Genoa* to escape London and find new sources of inspiration – and also because life in Italy was considerably cheaper. Dickens, although at first taken aback by the decay of the Ligurian capital, appears to have been fascinated by this new country and a quick learner of its language and customs. He did not write much there, apart from another Christmas book, *The Chimes*, the publication of which occasioned a brief return to London. In all the Dickenses remained in Italy for a year, travelling around the country for three months in early 1845, before returning to England in July of that year.

In Italy, he discovered that he was apparently able mesmerically to alleviate the condition of Augusta de la Rue, the wife of a Swiss banker, who suffered from anxiety and nervous spasms. This treatment required him to spend a lot of time alone with her, and unsurprisingly Catherine was not best pleased by this turn of events. She was also worn out by the burden of motherhood: they were becoming a large family, and would eventually have a total of ten children. Catherine's sister Georgina therefore began to help out with the children. Georgina was in many ways similar to Mary, whose death had so devastated Dickens, and she became involved with Dickens's various projects.

Back in London, Dickens took part in amateur theatrical productions, and took on the task of editing the *Daily News*, a new national newspaper owned by Bradbury and Evans. However, he had severely underestimated the work involved in editing the publication and resigned after seventeen issues, though he did continue to write contributions, including a series of 'Travelling Letters' – later collected in *Pictures from Italy* (1846).

More Travels Perhaps to escape the aftermath of his resignation from the *Daily*
Abroad *News* and to focus on composing his next novel, Dickens moved his family to Lausanne in Switzerland. He enjoyed the clean, quiet and beautiful surroundings, as well as the company of the town's fellow English expatriates. He also managed to write fiction: another Christmas tale entitled *The Battle of Life* and, more significantly, the beginning of *Dombey and Son*, which began serialization in September 1846 and was an immediate success.

It was also at this point that his publisher launched a series of cheap editions of his works, in the hope of tapping into new markets. Dickens returned to London, and resumed his normal routine of socializing, amateur theatricals, letter-writing and public speaking, and also became deeply involved in charitable work, such as setting up and administering a shelter for homeless women, which was funded by Miss Burdett-Coutts. *The Haunted Man*, another Christmas story, appeared in 1848, and was followed by his next major novel, *David Copperfield* (1849–50), which received rapturous critical acclaim.

Household *Household Words* was set up at this time, a popular magazine
Words founded and edited by Dickens himself. The magazine contained fictional work by not only Dickens, but also contributors such as Gaskell and Wilkie Collins, and articles on social issues. Dickens continued with his amateur theatricals, which proved a welcome distraction, since Catherine was quite seriously ill, as was his father, who died shortly afterwards. This was followed by the sudden death of his eight-month-old daughter Dora.

The Dickenses moved house again in November 1851, this time to Tavistock House in Tavistock Square. Since it was in a dilapidated state, renovation was necessary, and Dickens personally supervised every detail of this, from the installation of new plumbing to the choice of wallpaper. *Bleak House* (1852–53), his next publication, sold well, though straight after finishing it, Dickens was in desperate need of a break. He went on holiday in France with his family, and then toured Italy with Wilkie Collins and the painter Augustus Egg. After his return to London, Dickens gave a series of public readings to larger audiences than he had been accustomed to. Dickens's histrionic talents thrived in this context and the readings were a triumph, encouraging the author to repeat the exercise throughout his career – indeed, this became a lucrative venture, with Dickens employing his friend Arthur Smith as his booking agent.

During this period Dickens's stance on current politics and society became increasingly critical, which manifested itself in the numerous satirical essays he penned and the darker, more trenchant outlook of *Bleak House* and the two novels that followed, *Hard Times* (1854) and *Little Dorrit* (1855–57). In March 1856, Dickens bought Gad's Hill Place, near Rochester, for use as a country home. He had admired it during childhood country walks with his father, who had told him he might eventually own it if he were very hard-working and persevering.

However, this acquisition of a permanent home was not accompanied by domestic felicity, as by this point Dickens's marriage was in crisis. Relations between Dickens and his wife had been worsening for some time, but it all came to a head when he became acquainted with a young actress by the name of Ellen Ternan and apparently fell in love with her. The affair may never have been consummated, but Dickens involved himself with Ellen and her family's life to an extent which alarmed Catherine, just as she had been alarmed by the excessive attentions he had paid to Mme de la Rue in Genoa. Soon enough, Dickens moved into a separate bedroom in their house, and in May 1858, Dickens and his wife formally separated. This gave rise to a flurry of speculation, including rumours that Dickens was involved in a relationship with the young actress, or even worse, his sister-in-law, Georgina Hogarth, who had opted to continue living with Dickens instead of with her sister. It seemed that some of these allegations may have originated from the Hogarths, his wife's immediate family, and Dickens reacted to this by forcing them to sign a retraction, and by issuing a public statement – against his friends' advice – in *The Times* and *Household Words*. Furthermore, in August of that year one of Dickens's private letters was leaked to the press, which placed the blame for the breakdown of their marriage entirely on Catherine's shoulders, accused her of being a bad mother and insinuated that she was mentally unstable. After some initial protests, Catherine made no further effort to defend herself, and lived a quiet life until her death twenty years later. She apparently never met Dickens again, but never stopped caring about him, and followed his career and publications assiduously.

This conflict in Dickens's personal affairs also had an effect on his professional life: in 1859 the author fell out with Bradbury and Evans after they had refused to run another statement about his private life in one of their publications, the satirical magazine

The End of the Marriage

All the Year Round

Punch. This led him to transfer back to Chapman and Hall and to found a new weekly periodical *All the Year Round.* His first contribution to the magazine was his highly successful second historical novel, *A Tale of Two Cities* (1859), an un-Dickensian work in that it was more or less devoid of comical and satirical elements. *All the Year Round* – which focused more on fiction and less on journalistic pieces than its predecessor – maintained very healthy circulation figures, especially as the second novel to be serialized was the tremendously popular *The Woman in White* by Wilkie Collins, who became a regular collaborator. Dickens also arranged with the New York publisher J.M. Emerson & Co. for his journal to appear across the Atlantic. In December 1860, Dickens began to serialize what would become one of his best-loved novels, the deeply autobiographical *Great Expectations* (1860–61).

Our Mutual Friend   Between the final instalment of *Great Expectations* and the first instalment of his next and final completed novel, *Our Mutual Friend*, there was an uncharacteristically long three-year gap. This period was marked by two deaths in the family in 1863: that of his mother – which came as a relief more than anything, as she had been declining into senility for some time, and Dickens's feeling for her were ambivalent at best – and that of his second son, Walter – for whom Dickens grieved much more deeply. He chewed over ideas for *Our Mutual Friend* for at least two years and only began seriously composing it in early 1864, with serialization beginning in May. Although the book is now widely considered a masterpiece, it met with a tepid reception at the time, as readers did not entirely understand it.

Staplehurst Train Disaster   On 9th June 1865, Dickens experienced a traumatic incident: travelling back from France with Ellen Ternan and her mother, he was involved in a serious railway accident at Staplehurst, in which ten people lost their lives. Dickens was physically unharmed, but nevertheless profoundly affected by it, having spent hours tending the dying and injured with brandy. He drew on the experience in the writing of one of his best short stories, 'The Signalman'.

Final Years   Following the success of his public readings in Britain, Dickens had been contemplating a tour of the United States, and finally embarked on a second trip to America from December 1867 to April 1868. This turned out to be a very lucrative visit, but the exhaustion occasioned by his punishing schedule proved to be disastrous for his health. He began a farewell tour around England in 1868, incorporating a spectacular piece derived from *Oliver Twist*'s scene of Nancy's murder, but was forced to abandon the tour on the instructions of his doctors after he had a stroke in April 1869. Against medical advice, he insisted on giving a series of twelve final readings in London in 1870. These were very well received, many of those who attended commenting that he had never read so well as then. While in London, he had a private audience with Queen Victoria, and met the Prime Minister.

Dickens immersed himself in writing another major novel, *The Mystery of Edwin Drood*, the first six instalments of which were a critical and financial success. Tragically this novel was never to be completed, as Dickens died on 9th June 1870, having suffered a stroke on the previous day. He had wished to be buried in a small graveyard in Rochester, but this was overridden by a nationwide demand that he should be laid to rest in Westminster Abbey. This was done on 14th June 1870, after a strictly private ceremony which he had insisted on in his will. *Death*

Charles Dickens's Works

As seen in the account of his life above, Charles Dickens was an immensely prolific writer, not only of novels but of countless articles, sketches, occasional writings and travel accounts, published in newspapers, magazines and in volume form. Descriptions of his most famous works can be found below.

Sketches by Boz, a revised and expanded collection of Dickens's newspaper pieces, was published in two volumes by John Macrone on 8th February 1836. The book was composed of sketches of London life, manners and society. It was an immediate success, and was praised by critics for the "startling fidelity" of its descriptions. *Sketches by Boz*

The first instalment of Dickens's first serialized novel, *The Pickwick Papers*, appeared in March 1836. Initially Dickens's contributions were subordinate to those of the illustrator Robert Seymour, but as the series continued, this relationship was inverted, with Dickens's writing at the helm. This led to an upsurge in sales, until *The Pickwick Papers* became a fully fledged literary phenomenon, with circulation rocketing to 40,000 by the final instalment in November 1837. The book centres around the Pickwick Club and its founder, Mr Pickwick, who travels around the country with his companions Mr Winkle, Mr Snodgrass and Mr Tupman, and consists of various loosely connected and light-hearted adventures, with hints of the social satire which would pervade his mature fiction. There is no overall plot, as Dickens invented one episode at a time and, reacting to popular feedback, would switch the emphasis to the most successful characters. *The Pickwick Papers*

Oliver Twist   Dickens's first coherently structured novel, *Oliver Twist*, was serialized in *Bentley's Miscellany* from February 1837 to April 1839, with illustrations by the famous caricaturist George Cruikshank. Subtitled *A Parish Boy's Progress*, in reference to Hogarth's *A Rake's Progress* and *A Harlot's Progress* cycles, Dickens tells the story of a young orphan's life and ordeals in London – which had never before been the substance of a novel – as he flees the workhouse and unhappy apprenticeship of his childhood to London, where he falls in with a criminal gang led by the malicious Fagin, before eventually discovering the secret of his origins. *Oliver Twist* publicly addressed issues such as workhouses and child exploitation by criminals – and this preoccupation with social ills and the plight of the downtrodden would become a hallmark of Dickens's fiction.

Nicholas   Dickens's next published novel – the serialization of which
Nickleby   for a while overlapped with that of *Oliver Twist* – was *Nicholas Nickleby*, which revolves around its eponymous hero – again an impoverished young man, though an older one this time – as he tenaciously overcomes the odds to establish himself in the world. When Nicholas's father dies penniless, the family turn to their uncle Ralph Nickleby for assistance, but he turns out to be a mean-spirited miser, and only secures menial positions for Nicholas and his sister Kate. Nicholas is sent to work in Dotheboys Hall, a dreadful Yorkshire boarding school administered by the schoolmaster Wackford Squeers, while Kate endures a humiliating stint at a London millinery. The plot twists and turns until both end up finding love and a secure position in life. Dickens's satire is more trenchant, particularly with regard to Yorkshire boarding schools, which were notorious at the time. Interestingly, within ten years of *Nicholas Nickleby*'s publication all the schools in question were closed down. Overall though, the tone is jovial and the plot is rambling and entertaining, much in the vein of Dickens's eighteenth-century idols Fielding and Smollett.

The Old   *The Old Curiosity Shop* started out as a piece in the short-lived
Curiosity Shop   weekly magazine that Dickens was editing, *Master Humphrey's Clock*, which began publication in April 1840. It was intended to be a miscellany of one-off stories, but as sales were disappointing, Dickens was forced to adapt the 'Personal Adventures of Master Humphrey' into a full-length narrative that would be the most Romantic and fairy-tale-like of Dickens's novels, with some of his greatest humorous passages. The story revolves around Little Nell, a young girl who lives with her grandfather in his eponymous shop, and recounts how the two struggle to release themselves from the
146   grip of the evil usurer dwarf Quilp. By the end of its serialization,

circulation had reached the phenomenal figure of 100,000, and Little
Nell's death had famously plunged thousands of readers into grief.

As seen above, Dickens took on a different genre for his next *Barnaby Rudge*
major work of fiction, *Barnaby Rudge*: this was a historical novel,
addressing the anti-Catholic Gordon riots of 1780, which focused
on a village outside London and its protagonist, a simpleton called
Barnaby Rudge. The novel was serialized in *Master Humphrey's
Clock* from 1840 to 1841, and met with a lukewarm reception from
the reading public, who thirsted for more novels in the vein of *The
Old Curiosity Shop*.

Dickens therefore gave up on the historical genre, and began serial- *Martin
izing the more picaresque *Martin Chuzzlewit* from December 1842 *Chuzzlewit*
to June 1844. The book explores selfishness and its consequences:
the eponymous protagonist is the grandson and heir of the wealthy
Martin Chuzzlewit senior, and is surrounded by relatives eager to
inherit his money. But when Chuzzlewit junior finds himself dis-
inherited and penniless, he has to make his own way in the world.
Although it was a step forwards in his writing, being the first of his
works to be written with a fully predetermined overall design, it sold
poorly – partly due to the fact that publishing in general was expe-
riencing a slump in the early 1840s. In a bid to revive sales, Dickens
adjusted the plot during the serialization and sent the title character
to America – his own recent visit there providing much material.

In 1843, Dickens had the idea of writing a small seasonal Christ- *Christmas
mas book, which would aim to revive the spirit of the holiday and *Books and
address the social problems that he was increasingly interested in. *The Haunted
The resulting work, *A Christmas Carol*, was a phenomenal suc- *House*
cess at the time, and the tale and its characters, such as Scrooge,
Bob Cratchit and Tiny Tim, have now achieved an iconic status.
Thackeray famously praised it as "a national benefit and to every
man or woman who reads it a personal kindness". Dickens published four more annual Christmas novellas – *The Chimes*, *The
Cricket on the Hearth*, *The Battle of Life* and *The Haunted Man*
– which were successful at the time, but did not quite live up to
the classic appeal of *A Christmas Carol*. After *The Haunted Man*,
Dickens discontinued his Christmas books, but he included annual
Christmas stories in his magazines *Household Words* and *All the
Year Round*. Each set of these stories usually took the form of a
miniature *Arabian Nights*, with a number of unrelated short stories
linked together through a frame narrative – typically Dickens wrote
the frame narrative, and invited other writers to supply the stories
included within it, writing the occasional one of them himself. *The
Haunted House* appeared in *All the Year Round* in 1862. 147

Dombey and Son   While living in Lausanne, Dickens composed *Dombey and Son*, which was serialized between October 1846 and April 1848 by Bradbury and Evans with highly successful results. The novel centres on Paul Dombey, the wealthy owner of a shipping company, who desperately wants a son to take over his business after his death. Unfortunately his wife dies giving birth to the longed-for successor, Paul Dombey junior, a sickly child who does not survive long. Although Dombey – who neglects his fatherly responsibilities towards his daughter Florence – is for the most part unsympathetic, he ends up turning a new leaf and becoming a devoted family man. Significantly, this is the first of Dickens's novels for which his working notes survive, from which one can clearly see the great care and detail with which he planned the novel.

David Copperfield   *David Copperfield* (1849–1850) is at once the most personal and the most popular of Dickens's novels. He had tried, probably during 1847–48, to write his autobiography, but, according to his own later account, had found writing about certain aspects, such as his first love for Maria Beadnell, too painful. Instead he chose to transpose autobiographical events into a first-person *Bildungsroman*, *David Copperfield*, which drew on his personal experience of the blacking factory, journalism, his schooling at Wellington House and his love for Maria. Its depiction of the Micawbers owed much to Dickens's own parents. There was great critical acclaim for the novel, and it soon became widely held to be his greatest work.

Bleak House   For his next novel, *Bleak House* (1852–53), Dickens turned his satirical gaze on the English legal system. The focus of the novel is a long-running court case, Jarndyce and Jarndyce, the consequences of which reach from the filthy slums to the landed aristocracy. The scope of the novel may well be the broadest of all of his works, and Dickens also experimented with dual narrators, one in the third person and one in the first. He was well equipped to write on the subject matter due to his experiences as a law clerk and journalist, and his critique of the judiciary system was met with recognition by those involved in it, which helped set the stage for its reform in the 1870s.

Hard Times   *Hard Times* was Dickens's next novel, serialized in *Household Words* between April and August 1854, in which he satirically probed into social and economic issues to a degree not achieved in his other works. Using the infamous characters Thomas Gradgrind and Josiah Bounderby, he attacks utilitarianism, workers' conditions in factories, spurious usage of statistics and fact as opposed to imagination. The story is set in the fictitious northern industrial setting of Coketown, among the workers, school pupils and teachers.

The shortest and most polemical of Dickens's major novels, it sold extremely well on publication, but has only recently been fully accepted into the canon of Dickens's most significant works.

Little Dorrit (1855–57) was also a darkly critical novel, satirizing the shortcomings of the government and society, with institutions such as debtor's prisons – in one of which, as seen above, Dickens's own father had been held – and the fantastically named Circumlocution Office bearing the brunt of Dickens's bile. The plot centres on the romance which develops between the characters of Little Dorrit, a paragon of virtue who has grown up in prison, and Arthur Clennam, a hapless middle-aged man who returns to England to make a living for himself after many years abroad. Although at the time many critics were hostile to the work, taking issue with what they saw as an overly convoluted plot and a lack of humour, sales were outstanding and the novel is now ranked as one of Dickens's finest.

A Tale of Two Cities is the second of Dickens's historical novels, covering the period between 1775 and 1793, from the American Revolution until the middle of the French Revolution. His primary source was Thomas Carlyle's *The French Revolution*. The story is of two men – Charles Darnay and Sydney Carton – who look very similar, though they are utterly different in character, who both love the same woman, Lucie Manette. The opening and closing sentences are among the most famous in literature: "It was the best of times, it was the worst of times." "It is a far, far better thing that I do, than I have ever done; it is a far, far better rest that I go to than I have ever known."

Due to a slump in circulation figures for *All the Year Round*, Dickens brought out his next novel, in December 1860, as a weekly serial in the magazine, instead of having it published in monthly instalments as initially intended. The sales promptly recovered, and the audience and critics were delighted to read the story which some regard as Dickens's greatest ever work, *Great Expectations* (1860–61). On publication, it was immediately acclaimed a masterpiece, and was hugely successful in America as well as England. Like *David Copperfield*, it was written in the first person as a *Bildungsroman*, though this time its protagonist, Pip, was explicitly working class. Graham Greene once commented: "Dickens had somehow miraculously varied his tone, but when I tried to analyse his success, I felt like a colour-blind man trying intellectually to distinguish one colour from another." George Orwell was moved to declare: "Psychologically the latter part of *Great Expectations* is about the best thing Dickens ever did."

Little Dorrit

A Tale of Two Cities

Great Expectations

Our Mutual Friend

Dickens started work on his next novel, *Our Mutual Friend* (1864–65), by 1861 at the latest. It had an unusually long gestation period, and a mixed reception when first published. However, in recent years it has been reappraised as one of his greatest works. It is probably his most challenging and complicated, although some critics, including G.K. Chesterton, have argued that the ending is rushed. It opens with a young man on his way to receive his inheritance, which he can apparently only attain if he marries a beautiful and mercenary girl, Bella Wilfer, whom he has never met. However, before he arrives, a body is found in the Thames, which is identified as being him. So instead the money passes on to the Boffins, the effects of which spread through to various parts of London society.

The Mystery of Edwin Drood

In April 1870, the first instalment of Dickens's last novel, *The Mystery of Edwin Drood*, appeared. It was the culmination of Dickens's lifelong fascination with murderers. It was favourably received, outselling *Our Mutual Friend*, but only six of the projected twelve instalments were published, as Dickens died in June of that year.

There has naturally been much speculation on how the book would have finished, and suggestions as to how it should end. As it stands, the novel is set in the fictional area of Cloisterham, which is a thinly veiled rendering of Rochester. The plot mainly focuses on the choirmaster and opium addict John Jasper, who is in love with Rosa Bud – his pupil and his nephew Edwin Drood's fiancée. The twins Helena and Neville Landless arrive in Cloisterham, and Neville is attracted to Rosa Bud. Neville and Edwin end up having a huge row one day, after which Neville leaves town, and Edwin vanishes. Neville is questioned about Edwin's disappearance, and John Jasper accuses him of murder.

Select Bibliography

Biographies:

Ackroyd, Peter, *Dickens* (London: Sinclair-Stevenson, 1990)

Forster, John, *The Life of Charles Dickens* (London: Cecil Palmer, 1872–74)

James, Elizabeth, *Charles Dickens* (London: British Library, 2004)

Kaplan, Fred, *Dickens: A Biography* (London: Hodder & Stoughton, 1988)

Smiley, Jane, *Charles Dickens* (London: Weidenfeld and Nicolson, 2002)

Additional Recommended Background Material:

Collins, Philip, ed., *Dickens: The Critical Heritage* (London: Routledge & Kegan Paul, 1971)

Fielding, K.J, *Charles Dickens: A Critical Introduction* 2nd ed. (London: Longmans, 1965)

Wilson, Angus, *The World of Charles Dickens* (London: Secker & Warburg, 1970)

On the Web:
dickens.stanford.edu
dickens.ucsc.edu
www.dickensmuseum.com

ALMA CLASSICS

ALMA CLASSICS aims to publish mainstream and lesser-known European classics in an innovative and striking way, while employing the highest editorial and production standards. By way of a unique approach the range offers much more, both visually and textually, than readers have come to expect from contemporary classics publishing.

LATEST TITLES PUBLISHED BY ALMA CLASSICS

To order any of our titles and for up-to-date information about our current and forthcoming publications, please visit our website on:

www.almaclassics.com